Anonymous

Reading-Book

NEW No. IV.

SALZWASSER VERLAG

Anonymous

Reading-Book

NEW No. IV.

Reprint of the original, first published in 1864.

1st Edition 2022 | ISBN: 978-3-75259-461-4

Verlag (Publisher): Salzwasser Verlag GmbH, Zeilweg 44, 60439 Frankfurt, Deutschland
Vertretungsberechtigt (Authorized to represent): E. Roepke, Zeilweg 44, 60439 Frankfurt, Deutschland
Druck (Print): Books on Demand GmbH, In de Tarpen 42, 22848 Norderstedt, Deutschland

NEW No. IV.

READING-BOOK.

Illustrated.

LONDON

1864.

PREFACE.

ADDRESSED TO TEACHERS AND PARENTS.

No principle has been more thoroughly established by recent experience, or is more generally insisted upon by intelligent Teachers and School Inspectors, than that good reading is more readily acquired by practice than by precept. Without under-rating the importance of the watchful care and supervision of a judicious Teacher, it may safely be affirmed that in this as in other things it is practice that makes perfect. The more children read, they will read the more fluently, the more intelligently, the more gracefully. How, then, are children to be induced to read much? Obviously by giving them subjects to read about in which they will naturally feel interested, and by so treating these subjects as to render them attractive.

It is with special reference to this principle, both as regards matter and style, that this Reading-Book has been prepared. It is a common error to suppose that it is easy to write for children. Nothing, really, is more difficult. Indeed it is nearly as hard for mature minds to write for young people, as it would be for children to write for the edification and instruction of their seniors. The ideal child's book would be a book written by a child; and the nearest approach to that ideal is a book written in whole or in part by those few men and women who have the special gift and knack of writing for children. It will not be denied that A. L. O. E. is one of those writers who possess this peculiar gift; in proof of which it is only necessary to refer to the lessons* in this volume which bear that favourite signature. It is the chief aim of the volume to train young people, not only in the art of

* It may be necessary to call the attention of the compilers of school-books to the fact that these lessons, as well as many of the selected passages, are the exclusive property of the Publishers.

reading, but to the love of it. It appeals, in the first instance, to the powers of observation and imagination; but it does not overlook the fact that it is through these faculties, in the case of children, that the judgment and reasoning powers are first reached, and the taste and moral sensibilities are first cultivated. The pieces selected are of a character well calculated to give life, and point, and fresh interest to the daily work of the class—to allure the children to read, and to make them delight in exercising their power of reading. They avoid as much as possible that dull solidity which so much tends to make school hours a weariness to the young.

The numerous Illustrations afford an important aid in this respect. The interest of children is far more readily quickened through the eye than through the understanding; indeed it is through the eye that the understanding itself is most quickly reached. Good pictures are amongst the best incentives both to reading and to thinking. Certainly he were a dull boy who could look upon the clever picture of the Sleeping Sailor surrounded by the Night-capped Monkeys at page 65, or of the Tiger at page 52, or of the Dog and Shadow at page 125, without wishing to know "all about it." It should not be overlooked, at the same time, that pictures like those in this volume, which are not only appropriate and instructive, but highly artistic, serve an important end in training the eye and cultivating the taste. Nearly the whole of these Illustrations have been designed and drawn specially for this book. They are therefore not merely pictures thrown in for the sake of convenience or variety—they are really illustrative of the lessons to which they are attached.

The Proverbs, Anecdotes, &c., scattered through the volume, will afford a pleasant change from the more continuous lessons; while the elliptical form in which many of them are given will exercise the ingenuity of the children, and encourage them to voluntary working,—truly the best assistant which the Teacher can have in the performance of his arduous duties.

August 1864.

CONTENTS.

*** *Those in Italics are Poetical Pieces.*

SECTION I.

SECTION II.

READING-LESSONS.

TIT FOR TAT.

sit′-ting	**mis′-chief**	**be-tween′**
eat′-ing	**win′-dow**	**mo′-ment**
hear′-ing	**fel′-low**	**stretched**
laugh′-ing	**knuc′-kles**	**mer′-ri-ly**

A BOY was one day sitting on the steps of a door. He had a broom in one hand, and a large piece of bread and butter, which somebody had kindly given him, in the other. While he was eating it, and merrily humming a tune, he saw a poor little dog quietly sleeping not far from him. He called out to him, "Come here, poor fellow!" The dog, hearing himself kindly spoken to, got up, pricked up his ears, wagged his tail, and seeing the boy eating, came near him. The boy held out to him a piece of his bread and butter; and as the dog stretched out his head to take it, the boy hastily drew back his hand and hit him a hard rap on the nose. The poor dog ran away howling most dreadfully, while the cruel boy sat laughing at the mischief he had done.

A gentleman, who was looking from a window on the other side of the street, saw what the wicked boy had done. Opening the street door, he called him to cross over, at the same time showing him a sixpence, which he held between his finger and thumb.

"Would you like this?" said the gentleman.

"Yes, if you please, sir," said the boy, smiling; and he hastily ran over to seize the prize.

Just at the moment that he stretched out his hand, he got so severe a rap on the knuckles, from a cane which the gentleman had behind him, that he roared out like a bull!

"What did you do that for?" said he, making a very long face, and rubbing his hand. "I didn't hurt you, nor ask you for the sixpence."

"What did you hurt that poor dog for just now?" said the gentleman. "He didn't hurt you, nor ask you for your bread and butter. As you served him I have served you. Now, remember dogs can feel as well as boys, and learn to behave kindly towards poor animals in future."

BRAVE BOBBY.

pas´sen-gers	leaped	col´lar
of´fi-cer	sud´den-ly	doub´led
frol´ic-some	a-long´side	al-low´ing
play´mate	re-cov´ered	lev´elled
grey´hound	sound´ed	shat´tered
fran´tic	New-found´land	hur-rah´

SOME years ago, a ship bound for China had on board, among other passengers, an officer, his wife, their only child a little boy five years old, and a large Newfoundland dog called Bobby.

Everybody in the ship liked Bobby, he was so good-tempered and frolicsome; but the little boy was the dog's constant play-mate. He was a merry little fellow, and as fond of Bobby as Bobby was of him.

One day while the little boy and the dog were romping together, the ship gave a roll, and splash went the child into the sea!

A cry was raised, "A hand over! a hand over!" and the brave dog sprang over the side of the ship, clearing it like a greyhound, and swam towards the stern.

The little boy's father, half frantic, leaped with others into the jolly-boat; but it was too dark to see far before them. All gave the child up for lost.

At last they heard a splash on the left side of the ship. "Pull on quick!" cried the father. The boat was turned, the men pulled with greater force, and in a moment brave Bobby, holding up the child with his mouth, was alongside! Joy! joy! joy!

The boat was rowed back to the ship; the half-drowned boy was recovered; the parents were delighted; and brave Bobby was patted and caressed by all.

At the Cape of Good Hope the passengers were to be landed. The officer got into the boat with his wife and child; but he told the sailors to hold the Newfoundland dog tight by the collar till the boat was some distance from the ship. "You will then see," said he, "what a strong swimmer he is." Brave Bobby pulled and tugged to get loose, but all in vain, for they held him till the boat was near the shore. No sooner did the officer give the signal than the dog was set at liberty, and away he went full dash into the sea.

Suddenly the poor animal set up a shrill howl, and threw himself out of the water. At first it was thought he had been seized with cramp; but it was worse than that—a shark was after him! "A shark! a shark!" sounded from the boat to the ship. Bobby swam right and left, and dived and doubled, showing his teeth, and never allowing the shark time to turn on his back, without doing which the monster could not bite him.

The officer in the boat soon saw that there was little chance of reaching the spot in time to save the dog. Poor Bobby swam and dodged, and was almost exhausted. "Stop rowing," cried the officer to the men, "and turn the boat round."

Just at this moment the shark, which had got very close to the dog, turned on his back and opened his horrid mouth!

Bobby was all but gone. His master rose, levelled his gun, and fired. In a moment the water was tinged with blood: the horrid jaws of the shark were shattered to pieces!

The men then rowed to the spot where Bobby was swimming about. The officer pulled the dog into the boat; the child threw his little arms around him; and the men in the boat and the sailors in the ship cried out with joy, "Hurrah! hurrah! joy! joy! Bobby is safe! the shark is killed! Hurrah! hurrah!"

THE DOG AT HIS MASTER'S GRAVE.

an′guish	**con-trolled′**	**of′fer-ings**
grave	**rus′tled**	**bu′ried**
guard′ed	**quiv′er-ing**	**moan′ing**
glowed	**mourn′ful**	**tomb′stone**
grate′ful	**pit′y-ing**	**strug′gled**

"*He will not come,*" said the gentle child,
And she patted the poor dog's head,
And she pleasantly called him and fondly smiled;
But he heeded her not in his anguish wild,
Nor arose from his lowly bed.

'Twas his master's grave where he chose to rest—
He guarded it night and day;

The love that glowed in his grateful breast,
For the friend who had fed, controlled, caressed,
Might never fade away.

And when the long grass rustled near,
Beneath some hasting tread,
He started up with a quivering ear,
For he thought 'twas the step of his master dear,
Returning from the dead.

But sometimes when a storm drew nigh,
And the clouds were dark and fleet,
He tore the turf with a mournful cry,
As if he would force his way, or die,
To his much-loved master's feet.

So there through the summer's heat he lay,
Till autumn nights grew bleak,
Till his eye grew dim with his hope's decay,
And he pined, and pined, and wasted away,
A skeleton gaunt and weak.

And oft the pitying children brought
Their offerings of meat and bread,
And to coax him away to their homes they sought;
But his buried master he ne'er forgot,
Nor strayed from his lonely bed.

Cold winter came with an angry sway,
And the snow lay deep and sore;

Then his moaning grew fainter day by day,
Till close where the broken tomb-stone lay,
He fell, to rise no more.

And when he struggled with mortal pain,
And Death was by his side,
With one loud cry that shook the plain,
He called for his master;—but called in vain,
Then stretched himself and died.

MRS. SIGOURNEY.

THE BOY WHO WAS ALWAYS TOO LATE.

planned	**la´zi-ly**	**chok´ing**
jour´ney	**an´swer**	**sulk´i-ly**
bright´ly	**snatch´ing**	**bus´iness**

SOLOMON SLOW was the son of a gentleman who lived on the border of the New Forest. His mother called him Solomon, "Because," said she, "he is a wise child; 'slow and sure' is sure to do well."

"Yes," said his father; "but he is too slow, and unless he become a little more quick, and a little less lazy, I shall never make a man of him."

When he was about ten years old, his father and some friends planned a pic-nic in the forest, and hired a large van for the journey. They were to set out at seven in the morning. Solomon knew this, as he heard his father say so the night before.

The sun was shining very brightly when he awoke at six the next morning, but he was as lazy as ever. "If I get up about ten minutes before seven," said he, "I shall be down in plenty of time." So he lay still in bed, and heard all the party pass his door as they went down stairs. They even called to him; but he gave no answer, and only lazily rolled himself up in the clothes. At last, up he jumped, dressed, and ran down stairs; but he found the breakfast-room empty, and the van gone! Snatching up his hat, he ran as fast as he could down the road; but there was a high wind, and the dust was in clouds everywhere. He screamed and bawled for the van to stop; but all in vain. No one could hear him; and at last, tired with running, and half choked with dust, he walked sulkily home.

But even this did not cure him. He was a lazy boy, and grew up to be a lazy man; and when in business, though the coach passed his door every

day, he was never ready. Just look at him, running up the hill, and bawling "Stop! stop!"

THE CAT.

PART I.

men-ag´e-rie	**pa´tience**	**foot´step**
leop´ard	**crouched**	**ac-count´a-ble**
ex-am´ine	**glit´ter-ing**	**phys´i-cal**
butch´er	**light´ning**	**struc´ture**

"WOULD it not be well first to know a little about the animals you are going to see at the menagerie next week?" said Mrs. Myrtle to her children. "Shall I tell you something about some of them till papa comes home? With which shall we begin?"

"With the camel," said Bessie.

"The great roaring lion," said Harry.

"What," said mamma, "if we should begin

with pussy, lying asleep there on the hearth-rug?"

The children, laughing, said, "We do not need to go to the menagerie to see pussy."

"True," said Mrs. Myrtle; "but as pussy is in most respects exactly like the great roaring lion, and the fierce tiger, and the spotted leopard, and is, in fact, of the same genus or kind, it will be easiest for us to examine her; for you would not like, I am pretty sure, to see a roaring lion spring up on my lap to have his teeth and claws looked at. But first tell me how pussy gets her food. What does she like best to eat?"

"Mice and birds," cried both the children at once.

"And does she catch them alive?"

"Oh, yes!"

"Then she does not need a butcher to kill her meat for her. She is a beast of prey. Have you ever seen her watch for a mouse?"

"Yes," said Harry; "if she can get into the store-closet she will sit a whole day watching for a mouse to stir."

"All the animals of her race," said Mrs. Myrtle, "are remarkable for the *patience* with which they wait and watch."

"But, mamma," said Bessie, "pussy is often very cruel. I saw something one day from a back window, which makes me dislike her every time I think of it. She had caught such a pretty little bird, and if she had eaten it up at once it would not have been so bad; but she let it get a good way off, and then crouched down and fixed her green eyes upon it, and it seemed not to be able to help looking at her. I thought it might have got off, if it had only spread its wings quickly and flown away; but she held it with her glittering eye, and they stood looking at each other such a time that my heart beat so loudly for the poor bird that I could hear it. But whenever it made a little flutter, she darted on it like lightning, and shook it in her mouth, and tossed it with her paws. Then she let it off again, and I thought this time I would try to save it. I ran quickly out, but whenever she heard my footsteps she seized it and darted off in a moment. Oh, *cruel* pussy!" said Bessie, looking reproachfully at the cat. But pussy, warm and comfortable, did not seem in the least conscious of the charges brought against her.

"My dear child," said Mrs. Myrtle, "you must remember that pussy has not a soul as you have; she is not at all aware of her cruelty. She wants the sense of right and wrong,—that which in human beings is called the *moral sense,* and which makes them accountable for their actions. She, on the other hand, has no choice. She *must* act according to her nature and *physical structure.*

"What is physical structure?" asked both the children.

"The way in which her body is made," replied their mother, "which fits her for a certain way of life. *You,* for example, could not, like puss, catch mice and birds, even if you were ever so willing, because your physical structure is entirely different. But let us proceed to examine Mistress Puss, and then you will see better what I mean. Lift her up gently on my knee."

Bessie and Harry made a cat's cradle of their little hands, and placed pussy where they were told. She purred a little, stretched herself, and lay down to sleep again.

THE CAT.

PART II.

cush´ion	**stir´ring**	**at´ti-tude**
vel´vet-y	**laugh´ing**	**in-tense´**
pierce	**scat´tered**	**mus´cles**
par´ti-cles	**rustl´ing**	**in-tes´tines**
di-lates´	**dis-tinc´tion**	**choos´ing**

"Now," said their mamma, "look first at her paws. Tell me how they are made."

"Oh!" said Harry, "they have a nice pad or cushion under each toe."

"And for what are these?" asked Mrs. Myrtle.

"I know," cried Bessie. "It is to make her tread softly, so that the mice and birds may not hear her when she goes to catch them."

"And are her paws always as soft and velvety as they are now?" asked mamma.

"No, indeed!" said Harry, laughing. "When I tease her, she puts out her sharp claws and gives me a good scratch."

"Do you think, then, these claws were given to her for nothing but to scratch you?"

"Oh! I dare say," said Bessie, "she puts them out when she makes her great jump, and catches hold of poor little mousey with them."

"Exactly so," said Mrs. Myrtle. "Without them the smooth skin of the mouse, or the shiny feathers of the birds, would slip out of her paws, which would be too soft and velvety to hold anything. Now hold back her head, open her mouth gently, and see what sort of teeth she has."

"She has," said the children, "four terrible ones at the corners, which must pierce like spears. She has back ones too, for eating with; but perhaps she kills and tears with the four long ones."

"Feel her tongue," said Mrs. Myrtle.

"We need not do that," replied the children; "she often licks our hands, and we know that her tongue is rough. What is that for?"

"It is that she may lick all the small particles of flesh clean off the bones, supposing that these should be too big for her to swallow. One thing more I shall point out to you, and that is her eyes. Do you know which part is the *pupil?*"

"Is it not the black thing in the middle?" asked Bessie.

"Yes; and that is just an opening for admitting the light. Now, if a great glare of light were to enter her eyes, she could make the pupils quite small, so as to shut it out. On the contrary, when there is very little light, she *dilates*, or opens them wide, in order to catch all that there is. It is this which enables her to find her food during the night; for the night is her natural time to be stirring and providing for herself. She cannot really see in total darkness; but in what seems darkness to us, she catches in those wide-opened pupils all the scattered rays of light. Her hearing, too, is very quick. I believe you will never catch her in so sound a sleep but that, if she hears the smallest rustling or chirping resembling that of a mouse or bird, she will instantly raise her head and listen."

"I have often seen her do that," said Bessie. "It is very curious to see her wake in a moment, prick up her ears, and listen with all her body."

"That is a very good distinction," said her mamma smiling. "If it were a human being, you would say "with all her soul;" but her attitude does give one the idea of an intense life pervading the whole being, which is altogether peculiar to her race. Now, when I tell you that every other part of her body is exactly and beautifully fitted for the same end—that is, to enable her to provide for her wants—you will see that her way of life is not of her own choosing. When you are old enough to study the subject further, you will know that all her muscles, all her bones, and all her *intestines*,—that is, her inward parts—are as exactly made and put together for one and the same end, as those which you can understand a little about even at present."

LION. LIONESS.

THE LION A GIANT CAT.

PART I.

ex-cla-ma´-tion	shag´-gy	con-fu´-sion
sur-prise´	buf´-fa-loes	pow´-er-less
stom´-ach	an´-te-lopes	earth´-quake
fe´-line	taw´-ny	shiv´-er-ing

"Now, mamma," said Harry, at the next lesson, "shall we have the great roaring lion this time?"

"Very well, darling, you shall," said his mamma; "but do you know that your great roaring lion is nothing more than a giant cat?"

The children uttered an exclamation of surprise.

"Yes, it is quite true," continued Mrs. Myrtle.

"Its teeth, its paws, its eyes, ears, stomach and all, are made quite like those of the cat; and it makes the same use of them—that is, it watches for its prey in the same still, patient manner, and then seizes it with an immense bound. Now you must try to remember that all animals of the cat kind are said to belong to the *feline race.*"

The children repeated this word over several times.

"Then," said Harry, "I suppose that the lions are the giants, and the real pussies are the dwarfs, among the cats. But the lions *look* very different in the pictures. They have great faces, large heavy heads, shaggy manes, and long tails with a tuft at the end."

"It is true that they *look* different," said Mrs. Myrtle. "The animals they prey upon being large and strong, such as deer, oxen, and buffaloes, they are more fitted to inspire terror than if they were in appearance merely great cats over again, ten or twelve feet long. Besides, God delights in making things different, and yet the same."

"*Different* and yet *the same!*" repeated the children; "how can that be?"

"You must think for a little while, both of you," said Mrs. Myrtle, "and then tell me whether you have found out *how that can be.*"

"Well," continued she, after a pause, "have you made it out?"

"The same," cried Harry eagerly, "if his skin were off! God has given the lion a different skin, and painted it differently."

"So far correct," said Mrs. Myrtle. "Bessie, what do you say?"

"The same," said Bessie, "in the chief things, such as his paws and teeth, and different in little things that are of no consequence."

"Very well, my dear," said Mrs. Myrtle; "only we cannot say of the smallest change that God makes that it is of *no consequence.* When we make changes in our dresses, for example, we do so *only* to please our fancy; but when God makes a change, be it ever so small, it not only pleases the fancy, but makes the animal or thing more surely and beautifully fit its own place in creation. Look at the lion's *painting,* for instance, and you will see that it is of much more consequence to him than the colour of a dress is to us. Although he likes to live and make his bed in the midst of thick bushes and tall underwood, yet, when he is hungry, he roams out over the wide sandy plains, where large herds of wild asses and antelopes go trooping along. Now these creatures are extremely swift—they run much faster than the lion: he seldom runs at all. They scent him at a distance, and feeling the utmost terror, they scour away over the desert like the wind; so that, if it were not that God had painted the lion of a tawny colour—that is, a reddish or yellowish brown—exactly like the sand over which he walks and where he couches, he could in some places hardly manage to get a morsel of food."

"But if they *scent* him, mamma," said Harry,

"how is it that they do not run out of his way when they can run so fast?"

"So they often do, and so they would always, but for the extreme terror which they feel, and which scatters them about in confusion, and makes them often run *to* him instead of running *from* him. Remember Bessie's bird, and how pussy 'held it with her glittering eye,' and you will see that extreme terror has a kind of charm in it which draws or renders powerless quite as much as it gives an impulse to run away. And no wonder the other animals feel in this manner, for in all creation there is not a more terrible object than an angry lion intent on his prey. He loves best those stormy nights when the thunder rolls along the skies, and the lightning flashes over the far desert wastes, while at intervals the rain pours down in dreadful torrents. By the light of those vivid flashes may be seen herds of trembling animals huddled together for shelter, while some instinct tells them that there is another enemy abroad more terrible than the storm. The great lion feels no fear. He walks alone in dread majesty. Suddenly he lays his mouth close to the ground, and utters a roar that makes the earth tremble, resembling the sound that accompanies an earthquake. The frightened animals know it well. They forsake each other, and seek in all directions to find safety in flight. Then the lion couches, his eye glares, and with one bound, or perhaps with several bounds, as rapid as the lightning, he fastens his teeth and claws in some shivering animal, and bears it away."

"Are there many lions roaming about in such nights," asked the children, looking a little frightened.

"They do not come very close together," replied Mrs. Myrtle; "for one lion requires a great district of country for the support of himself, his wife, and his one or two cubs—he never has more. But the deserts of Africa, where the lion reigns as king, are so vast that there must be a great many abroad in one night. You can hardly comprehend the immensity of those deserts, but look at the map, and you will see how large a part of the continent of Africa they cover. The lion lives also in Asia, but it is said that there he is less strong and courageous, and of a paler colour."

THE LION A GIANT CAT.

PART II.

Hot´-ten-tots	**wealth**	**drow´-sy**
neigh´-bour-ing	**ac-count´-ed**	**moon´-light**
sal´-lies	**con´-quered**	**star´-light**
plen´-ti-ful	**en-deav´-our**	**mut´-ter-ing**
cer´-e-mo-ny	**con-cealed´**	**cour´-age**
vis´-i-tors	**sun´-shine**	**as-sail´-ant**

"The Arabs in the north of Africa, and the Hottentots in the south, live in equal fear and dread of the lion. The Arabs, you know, dwell in tents; and when a number of these tents are put up near each other, so as to make a little village, they call it a *douar.* Well, every night a lion will come and attack one of these douars, —not always the same, but sometimes one and sometimes another. He makes his home in one of the neighbouring mountains, perhaps twenty or thirty miles away. A nice well-kept home it is, under the thickest cover he can find. He clears several pieces of ground for rooms or chambers, and will not allow so much as a stone or a bit of stick to litter the ground. Here he lies snugly all day, and sleeps with his wife and little ones; but as soon as sunset comes, he sallies forth to seek food for himself and his family. Thirty or forty miles are only a nice walk for him. Down he marches from his mountain home, sometimes uttering a roar which is heard at an immense distance, and then all the animals begin to fly, generally in the direction of the Arab tents, wanting to find protection from man. That is not wise, however; for the lion, knowing very well where he is likely to find the most plentiful meal, makes directly for one of the tent villages. What confusion and terror there are then! All the animals —horses, oxen, camels—come rushing into the tents without ceremony, trampling upon and overturning women and children, while the dogs bark, the women scream, and the men light fires all around, and toss about flaming torches to try to scare the lion away. He minds them very little.

The thunder of his voice drowns all their noise, and he walks straight on to the place where he intends to make his choice, and will there slaughter three or four bulls or oxen at once. Sometimes he will drive one or two home before him all the way to his den, where his cubs are no doubt expecting such welcome visitors. The Arabs very seldom fire on the lion, because they have an idea that it is when made angry that he is most likely to attack men; so they just let themselves be plundered and ruined at his majesty's good pleasure. Some of them have had their flocks and herds, in which their wealth consists, carried entirely off.

"Some very dreadful stories are told about this most terrible of animals when he is enraged by any attempt to resist him. An Arab once watched for him inside the hedge which enclosed his tent village, and fired just at the moment when he was bounding across. Although the lion's shoulder was broken by the shot, this did not prevent him from tearing the man to pieces in a single moment. He then killed all who were in the tent except one woman, who managed to get out with her child in her arms, and who had reached the top of a neighbouring tent in safety, when the lion got hold of her by the leg just as she was drawing it up, and killed both her and her child. At the same time the weight of his body broke down the tent below, and not content with what he had already done, such was his rage, that he tore to pieces through the canvas every moving creature that gave sign of life. The person who relates this story, and who knows the lion better, and has seen him face to face oftener than any other man, is a French soldier named Gerard. He has been called the Lion-killer; for when he was in the north of Africa with the French army, which conquered a great part of that country, he made it the business of his life to endeavour to free the Arabs from this dreaded night-visitor.

"Formerly it had been the custom to dig a deep pit by the way-side, cover it with branches and brush-wood, and to lie concealed there in order to get a shot at the lion as he passed; or else his footsteps were tracked to his sleeping-place during the day, and he was surrounded and baited by dogs till he was aroused from his slumbers. This was by far the least dangerous way, because he dislikes exceedingly the glare of sunshine, probably not seeing very clearly in it; and besides, he feels drowsy after his heavy meal and his long walk, and wants very much to be alone to rest himself. Gerard, however, being a very brave man, went out alone in the moonlight or starlight nights, tracked the lion's footsteps, and waited for him night after night as patiently as the lion himself watches for his prey. Then, when he heard the heavy footstep and the muttering roar which bespoke his enemy at hand, he placed himself directly in his path, let him come as near as twelve or twenty paces, looked steadfastly into his face, into his glaring, fiery eyes, and then, just as he was going to spring, shot him directly through the forehead. It needed very great courage for a man to do this, because, if his first and second shot had missed the lion's brain or his heart, there would have been no time to fire again, and without doubt his assailant would have been torn to pieces. Gerard killed in this manner as many as twenty lions."

THE LION A GIANT CAT.

PART III.

south´ern	**cour-a´geous**	**for-bear´ing**
kraals	**u´ni-corn**	**car-a-van´**
set´tlers	**bla´zoned**	**pri´va-cy**
char´ac-ter	**gen-er-os´i-ty**	**trig´gers**

"I should like," said Harry, "to see on the map the place where the French army conquered, and where Gerard killed the lions."

"Here it is, my dear. Now, look down at the southern part of Africa. There live black people called *Hottentots*; and it was once said that the lion preferred the flesh of a Hottentot to that of any living creature. He often watched in the neighbourhood of their *kraals*—which is the name given to *their* villages of little miserable huts—to see if he could carry a man away. The Dutch settlers, who are people that have gone out from Holland to live there, say that the lion has now become afraid in some measure of the sound of fire-arms. I suppose it is for this reason that some books of natural history, lately published, have gone so far as to call him a coward, and to say that he is not worthy any longer to be considered the king of beasts. I am glad that Gerard has quite cleared his character from this charge, for in the lion he always met a courageous and noble enemy; and I am glad, partly because, as you know, he supports the royal arms of England."

"Oh, I know!—the lion and the unicorn fighting for the crown," said Harry.

"Yes; and there is a lion too blazoned on the royal shield of Scotland. He has been adopted by both countries as the emblem of courage and generosity. I will tell you a story to show that, terrible as we have found him to be, and savage in his anger, he is not always cruel, but, on the contrary, is often patient, forbearing, and generous."

"Do tell us a story, mamma," said Harry; "I like the stories."

"And I," said Bessie, "like to hear about the good parts in an animal's character."

"Very well," said mamma, "I hope to please you both. Dr. Burchell, who lived in South Africa, tells us that one bright day he was travelling with a caravan along the side of a river whose banks were covered with tall mat-rushes. His dogs began barking furiously at some concealed object, and soon a lioness and an enormous black-maned lion came into view. The lioness bounded away under cover of the rushes, but the lion came forward and stood still, gazing quite steadily, as if to say, 'Who are you that have dared to intrude on my privacy, and disturb my royal slumbers?' He was but a very few paces distant; many of the party were unarmed, and you may be sure did not feel very easy under the lion's gaze; but those who had guns put their fingers on the triggers that they might be ready to shoot. Dr. Burchell himself, who was on foot, having given his horse to some one in charge, held his pistols in the same manner. The brave dogs, still barking, rushed in between the men and the lion; but he took no notice of them, until two of them ventured to go close to his feet, when he slightly moved his paw, and in an instant those two were still in death! That terrible paw can with one stroke break a horse's back; and when he killed those dogs without turning his head, or even looking at them, Dr. Burchell could scarcely perceive how it was done. The men fired. A ball entered the lion's side, and the blood began to flow; but he still remained fixedly looking. They now expected every moment that he would spring upon them; but instead of doing so, he walked calmly away."

THE RAIN LESSON.

re-joice′	out-stretched′	lis′ten-ing
droop′ing	wil′der-ness	dis-ap-point′ment
mourn′er	ag′o-ny	ab-sorbed′
trav′el-ler	breathed	bright′en

"MOTHER, it rains!" and tears like rain fell down.
"O little daughter! see, the plants rejoice;
The rose-buds blush, and in your garden-bed
The drooping violets look so gladly up,
Blessing our God for rain. He knows what's best.

"Yes, mother, He knows everything; and so
He surely knows there's but one afternoon
In all the week that I can have from school;
And 'tis the third that I've had leave to go
And play with Mary, if it did not rain,
And gather wild-flowers in her father's grove,
And now it rains again."

The mother took
The mourner on her knee, and kissed away
The blinding grief. And then she told her tales
Of the great Eastern deserts parched and dry,
And how the trav'ller 'mid the burning sands
Watches for rain-clouds with a fainting gaze;
And showed her pictures of the caravan,
And the poor camel with his outstretched neck
Longing for water.

And she told her, too,
Of the sad mother in the wilderness,
And the spent water-bottle:—how she laid
Her darling son among the shrubs to die,

Bowing her head down that she might not see
The agony of the long death from thirst;
And how the blessed Angel, when she prayed,
Showed her a crystal well to save her child.

And other stories from the Book of God
Breathed that kind teacher to the listening one
Seated so meek beside her:—how there fell
No rain in Israel, till the grass decayed,
And the brooks wasted, and the cattle died;
And good Elijah with his earnest prayer
Besought the Lord, till the consenting cloud
Gave rain, and thankful earth her fruits restored.

And then they sang a hymn; and full of joy,
The baby, crowing from his nurse's arms,
Came in and joined them, creeping merrily
After his little sister; till her pain
Of disappointment all absorbed in love,
She thanked her mother for the pleasant time
And for her tender lessons.

So that night,
Amid her simple prayer, they heard her say
Words of sweet praise to Him whose mercy gives
The blessed rain:—"For now I know, O God,
What pleases Thee is best."

O mother! seek
Ever, through cloud and sunshine, thus to lead
Thy little ones to love Him; so the tear
Shall brighten like the rainbow here, and gleam
At last a pearl-drop in thy crown of life.

MRS. SIGOURNEY.

RED AND BLACK.

sov´er-eign	**brought**	**sol´dier**
boat´ing	**un´der-tak-er**	**con-tra-dict´ed**
dig´ging	**crea´tures**	**at-tract´ed**

"HURRAH for the sea-side!" cried Phil; "what fun I shall have with the boating and bathing, and digging away in the sand! But the fishing will be the best fun of all; many a jolly red lobster will I drag out of the sea!"

"*Red* lobsters!" exclaimed Bill, with a loud, rude laugh; "you will be clever to catch them! If you had ever seen a lobster, as I have seen many brought in the fishermen's baskets, you would have known that the creatures with their strong big claws are pretty nearly *black*."

"None of your nonsense for me!" cried Phil; "as if I didn't know the look of a lobster, when my aunt has lobster-salad twenty times in the year! The shell is as red as a soldier's coat!"

"As black as an undertaker's!" laughed Bill.

Phil was so angry at being thus contradicted, that he began to look almost as red as a lobster himself. From high words the two boys were almost coming to blows, when, attracted by their loud voices, Bill's grandfather drew near.

"Hollo! what's the matter?" said he.

"Grandfather, are not lobsters black?" cried Bill.

"Are they not red?" shouted out his companion.

"Ah, my lads," said the old man, "how often it is our own ignorance that makes us believe that no one knows the truth so well as ourselves! Neither of you, it seems, is aware that lobsters are black *until boiled*, and that then their colour is changed. I would give Phil a sovereign for any *red* lobster that he could fish out of the sea, and Bill another for any *black* one that he could eat at the table."

A. L. O. E.

THE BLIND BOY.

re-plied′	**dear′-est**	**prayed**
sighed	**thought**	**sight′-less**
leaves	**dis-ease′**	**sweet′-ly**
fra′-grant	**wid′-owed**	**o′-pened**

"DEAR Mary," said the poor blind boy,
"That little bird sings very long;
Say, do you see him in his joy,
And is he pretty as his song?"

"Yes, Edward, yes," replied the maid;
"I see the bird on yonder tree."
The poor boy sighed, and gently said,—
"Sister, I wish that I could see.

The flow'rs, you say, are very fair,
And bright green leaves are on the trees,
And pretty birds are singing there—
How beautiful for one who sees!

Yet I the fragrant flow'rs can smell;
  And I can feel the green leaf's shade;
And I can hear the notes that swell
  From those sweet birds that God has made.

So, sister, God to me is kind,
  Though sight, alas! He has not given;—
But tell me, are there any blind
  Among the children up in heaven?"

"No, dearest Edward, there all see;
  But why ask me a thing so odd?"—
"O Mary! He's so good to me
  I thought I'd like to look at God."

Ere long, Disease his hand had laid
  On that dear boy, so meek and mild:
His widowed mother wept and prayed
  That God would spare her sightless child.

He felt her warm tears on his face,
  And said,—"Oh! never weep for me;
I'm going to a better place,
  Where God my Saviour I shall see.

And you'll be there, dear Mary, too;—
  But, mother, when you get up there,
Tell me, dear mother, that 'tis you—
  You know I never saw you here."

He spoke no more, but sweetly smiled,
  Until the final blow was given,
When God took up that poor blind child,
  And opened first his eyes in heaven.

THE STONE THAT REBOUNDED.

prob′a-bly	**re-bound′**	**pois′ing**
pleas′ant	**ac′cu-rate**	**in′no-cent**
de-light′ful	**wel′comed**	**grieved**
friends	**con′fi-dence**	**con′science**

"O BOYS, boys, don't throw stones at that poor bird," said an old, gray-headed man.

"Why, sir," said a little fellow, "she makes such a squalling that we can't bear her."

"Yes; but she uses such a voice as God gave her, and it is probably as pleasant to her friends as yours is to those who love you. And, besides, that hoarse, flat voice, is not her only song. Early in a pretty morning you may hear her on some high tree, pouring out notes that are delightful. She often fills the air far and near with her varied and sweet melody. And I have yet another reason why I wish you not to stone her. I am afraid the stone will rebound, and hurt you as long as you live!"

"Rebound! We don't understand you, sir!"

"Well, come and I will tell you a story."

"Is it a *true* story?"

"Yes; every word is true."

"Fifty years ago I was a boy like you. I used to throw stones, and as I had no other boy very near me to play with, I threw them till I became very accurate in my aim. One day I went to work for an aged couple of the name of

Hamilton. They seemed very old people then. They were very kind to everybody and everything. Few had so many swallows making their nests under the roofs of their barns; few had so many pets that seemed to love them as they. For seven years a bird had come, after the long winter was over, and built her nest in the same place, and there reared her young ones. She had just returned on the day that I went there to work, and they welcomed her back. She hopped about, as if glad to get back. In the course of the day I thought I would try my skill upon her. She sat upon a post near the spot where she was to build her nest, and looked at me with all confidence, as much as to say, 'You won't hurt me?' I found a nice stone, and poising my arm, I threw it with my utmost skill. It struck the bird on the head, and she dropped dead! I was sorry the moment I saw her fall. But the deed was done. All day long her mate flew about, and chirped in tones so sad that he made my heart ache. Why had I taken a life so innocent, and made the poor mate grieve so? I said nothing to the old people about it. But through a grandchild they found it out; and, though they never said a word to me about it, I knew that they mourned for the bird, and were deeply grieved at my cruelty. I could never look them in the face afterwards as I had done before. Oh, that I had told them how sorry I was! They have been dead many, many years, and so has the poor bird; but don't you see how that stone *rebounded* and hit me? How deep a wound it made upon my memory!—how deep upon my conscience! Why, my dear boys, I would make great sacrifices to-day if I could undo that one deed! For fifty years I have carried it in my memory, and though I have never spoken of it before, yet if what I have now said shall prevent you from throwing a stone at a poor bird, that may rebound and deeply wound your conscience, I shall rejoice."

The boys thanked the aged man, dropped their stones, and the bird had no more trouble from them.

THE BETTER LAND.

ra´di-ant	**feath´er-y**	**di´a-mond**
or´ange	**glit´ter-ing**	**sor´row**
myr´tle	**fra´grant**	**breathe**
boughs	**per-fume´**	**fade´less**

"I HEAR thee speak of the better land,
Thou call'st its children a happy band;
Mother, oh! where is that radiant shore?
Shall we not seek it, and weep no more?
Is it where the flower of the orange blows,
And the fire-flies glance through the myrtle boughs?"
"Not there, not there, my child!"

"Is it where the feathery palm-trees rise,
And the date grows ripe under sunny skies?
Or 'midst the green islands on glittering seas,
Where fragrant forests perfume the breeze,
And strange bright birds, on their starry wings,
Bear the rich hues of all glorious things?"
"Not there, not there, my child!"

"Is it far away in some region old,
Where the rivers wander o'er sands of gold;
Where the burning rays of the ruby shine,
And the diamond lights up the secret mine,
And the pearl gleams forth from the coral strand;
Is it there, sweet mother, that better land?"
"Not there, not there, my child!—

"Eye hath not seen it, my gentle boy!
Ear hath not heard its deep songs of joy;
Dreams cannot picture a world so fair;
Sorrow and death may not enter there:
Time doth not breathe on its fadeless bloom;
For beyond the clouds and beyond the tomb—
It is there, it is there, my child!"

MRS. HEMANS.

TRY AGAIN

PART I.

fin´-ished	ear´-nest-ly	de-ceiv´-ing
en-gaged´	per-se-vere´	com-pan´-ion
dif´-fi-cult	thir´-ti-eth	whis´-pered
rea´-son	al´-pha-bet	en-cour´-ag-ing

"HAVE you finished your lesson, George?" said Mr. Prentice to his son, who had laid aside his book and was busily engaged making a large paper kite.

"No, father," replied George, hanging down his head.

"Why not, my son?"

"Because it is so difficult, father. I am sure that I shall never learn it."

"And what is the reason that you cannot learn it?"

"Because—because, I can't."

"Can't learn, George!"

"Indeed I have tried my best," replied the boy earnestly, the tears starting to his eyes; "but it is of no use, father. Other boys can get their lessons without any trouble. But I try, and try, and still I cannot learn them."

"*Cannot* is a word a boy should never utter, in speaking of his lessons. You *can* learn anything you please, George, if you only persevere."

"But have I not tried, and tried, father?"

"Yes, but you must try again."

"And so I have, father."

"Well, try again, and again; never say you cannot learn a lesson."

"But then I cannot remember it after I have learned it, my memory is so bad," urged the lad.

"If I were to promise you a holiday on the thirtieth of the month after the next, do you think you would forget it?"

"No, I am pretty sure that I should not."

"And why, George?"

"I cannot tell the reason; but I know I should remember it."

"Well, I can tell you. The pleasure of having a holiday would keep the date of it fresh in your memory. Now, if you were to take the same delight in learning that you do in playing, you would find no difficulty. You play at marbles well, I believe?"

"O yes, father, I beat every boy at school!"

"And your brother tells me that your kite flies highest, and that you are first in skating."

"Yes, my kite always flies the best; and I can cut every figure from one to nine and form every letter in the alphabet on the ice."

"You are very fond of skating, and flying your kite, and playing at ball and marbles?"

"Yes, father."

"And yet you cannot learn your lesson! My dear boy, you are deceiving yourself. You can learn as well as any one, if you will only try."

"But have I not tried, father?" again urged George.

"Well, try again. Come, for this afternoon lay

aside that kite you are making, and give another effort to get your lesson ready. Be in earnest, and you will soon learn it. To show you that it only requires perseverance, I will tell you a story :—

"One of the dullest boys at a village school, more than thirty years ago, went up to repeat his lesson one morning; and, as usual, did not know it. 'Go to your seat!' said the teacher angrily. 'If you don't pay more attention to your lessons you will never be fit for anything.'

"The poor boy stole off to his seat, and bent his eyes again upon his lesson.

"'It is of no use; I cannot learn,' he said in a whisper to a companion who sat near him.

"'You must try hard,' replied the kind-hearted boy.

"'I have tried, but it is of no use; I may just as well give up at once.'

"'*Try again,* Henry!' whispered his companion, in an earnest and encouraging tone.

TRY AGAIN.

PART II.

sen´-ten-ces	**im´-pulse**	**gath´-ered**
mas´-tered	**school´-mate**	**tire´-some**
pro-ceed´-ed	**ap-pli-ca´-tion**	**stead´-i-ly**
teach´-er	**cheer´-ful-ly**	**de-ter-mi-na´-tion**

"These two little words gave him a fresh impulse, and he bent his mind again to his task. It was only a simple grammar lesson—not difficult by any means. Gradually he began to find the sentences lingering in his memory; and soon, to his surprise and pleasure, the whole lesson was mastered! With a livelier motion and a more confident manner than he had ever before shown in going up to say a lesson, he rose from his seat and proceeded to the teacher's desk.

"'What do you want now?' asked the teacher

"'To say my lesson, sir.'

"'Did you not try half an hour ago?'

"'Yes; but I *can* say it now, sir,' timidly urged the boy.

"'Go on, then.'

"Henry commenced, and repeated the whole lesson without missing a word. The master gave him a look of pleasure as he handed him back his book, but said nothing. As the boy returned to his seat his step was lighter, for his heart beat with a new impulse.

"'Did you say it?' whispered his kind-hearted school-mate.

"'Every word!' replied the boy proudly.

"'Then you see you can learn.'

"'Yes, but it is hard work.'

"'But there is nothing like trying.'

"'No; and from this hour,' replied Henry, firmly, 'I will never say I cannot.'

"From that day," continued Mr. Prentice, "there was no boy in the school who learned more rapidly than Henry. It required much thought and application; but these he gave cheerfully, and success crowned his efforts."

"And did he always continue thus to learn?" asked George, looking up into his father's face.

"From that day till the present hour he has been a student; and he now urges his son George to 'try again,' as he tried."

"And was it indeed *you*, father?" asked his son, agerly looking up into the face of his kind parent.

"Yes, my child. That dull boy was your own father in his early years."

"Then I *will* try again," said George, in a decided tone; and, flinging aside his half-made kite, he turned and re-entered the house, and was soon bending in earnest attention over his lesson.

"Well, what success, George?" asked Mr. Prentice, as the family gathered around the tea-table.

"I learned the lesson, father!" replied the boy. "I can say every word of it."

"Did you find it hard work?"

"Not so very hard, after I had once made up my mind that I *would* learn it. Indeed I never stopped to think, as I usually do, about it being difficult or tiresome, but went right on until I had mastered every sentence."

"May you never forget this lesson, my son!" said Mr. Prentice, feelingly. "You possess now the secret of success. It lies in never stopping to think about a task being difficult or tiresome, but in going steadily on with a fixed determination to succeed."

ELLIPTICAL EXERCISES.

*** The following are all the words required in this page. The pupil must find out the right word for each blank space.**

wild	**know**	**replied**	**sent**
moment	**adventures**	**friends**	**answered**
thought	**people**	**fattens**	**schoolmaster**
surprise	**nothing**	**ran**	**scholars**

THE LATIN FOR COLD.

A . . . . asked one of his . . . . in the winter time what was the Latin word for cold.

"Oh, sir," . . . . the boy, "I forget it at this . . . . . . , but I have it at my fingers' ends.

A SLY HIT.

JOHN was . . . . to be very stupid. He was . . . . to a mill one day, and the miller said, "John, some . . . . . . say you are a fool. Now tell me what you . . . . and what you don't know."

"Well," . . . . John, "I know millers' hogs are fat!"

"Very well, John. Now tell me what you don't know."

"I don't know," said John, "whose corn . . . . them."

TRUTH AND FICTION

A TRAVELLER relating his . . . . to some friends, told them that he and his servant had once made fifty . . . . Arabs run. His . . . . stared in . . . . , but he told them there was . . . . wonderful in it after all. "For," says he, "we . . . and they . . . after us."

HAPPINESS.

"WERE I but a king," said a . . . . boy, "I would eat my fill of fat bacon, and . . . . . upon a . . . . all day long."

ELLIPTICAL EXERCISES.

WORDS PRONOUNCED ALIKE, BUT SPELT DIFFERENTLY.

*** The correct spelling of the word for each blank space either to be given orally or to be written on the slate.

awl all	. . . the poor shoemaker had was an . . . and some lasts. I did . . . I could to help him.
an Ann	. . . exchanged with little Emma . . apple for . . egg at the picnic.
blue blew	The wind . . . . away the sheet of . . . . paper, and it fell into the stream.
bough bow	. . . down, or you will strike your head against the . . . . . of the tree.
bad bade	If he . . . . you do so, he gave you . . . advice, and you should not follow it.
beet beat	He . . . . the poor dog with a . . . . root, and deserves to be . . . . himself.
buy by	. . next Christmas he will . . . something for you, and bring it when he comes.
bare bear	The . . . . tore his . . . . leg in such a manner that I could not . . . . to look at it.
beach beech	I have been told that . . . . .-trees seldom grow near the sea- . . . . .
bean been	I have . . . . looking at the . . . .-stalk, and it seems to be growing beautifully.
bread bred	These plump chickens were . . . . up on a sort of food like rye . . . . .
eight ate	The boys and girls . . . twenty . . . . . pears and . . . . . apples at the picnic.
feet feat	In performing the . . . . of jumping a fence five . . . . high he hurt one of his . . . .
forth fourth	On the . . . . . . of June we went . . . . . to meet them, and all returned together.
grown groan	Why do you . . . . . so? You have . . . . . very stout, and seem hardly able to walk.

THE ARK AND THE DOVE.

del´uge	**pin´ion**	**wan´der-ing**
re-fused´	**bound´less**	**wea´ried**
thith´er	**des-o-la´tion**	**lis´ten-er**
safe´ty	**dis-o-be´di-ence**	**love´li-ness**
cease´less	**peace´ful**	**e-ven´ing**
case´ment	**right´eous**	**ear´li-est**

In the following lines a mother relates how she told the story of the Ark and the Dove to her little girl :—

"Tell me a story, please," my little girl
Lisped from her cradle. So I bent me down,
And told her how it rained and rained and rained,
Till all the flowers were covered, and the trees

Hid their tall heads, and where the houses stood
And people dwelt, a fearful deluge rolled;
Because the world was wicked, and refused
To heed the words of God.

But one good man,
Who long had warned the wicked to repent,
Obey, and live, taught by the voice of Heaven,
Had built an ark; and thither, with his wife
And children, turned for safety.

Two and two,
Of beasts and birds and creeping things, he took,
With food for all; and, when the tempest roared,
And the great fountains of the sky poured out
A ceaseless flood, till all beside were drowned,
They in their quiet vessel dwelt secure.

And so the mighty waters bore them up,
And o'er the bosom of the deep they sailed
For many days. But then a gentle dove
'Scaped from the casement of the ark, and spread
Her lovely pinion o'er that boundless wave.

All was desolation. Chirping nest,
Nor face of man, nor living thing she saw;
For all the people of the earth were drowned,
Because of disobedience.

Naught she spied,
Save wide, dark waters, and a frowning sky,
Nor found her weary foot a place of rest:
So, with a leaf of olive in her mouth,
Sole fruit of her drear voyage, which perchance

Upon some wrecking billow floated by,
With drooping wing the peaceful ark she sought.

The righteous man that wand'ring dove received,
And to her mate restored, who, with sad moans,
Had wondered at her absence.

Then I looked
Upon the child, to see if her young thoughts
Wearied with following mine. But her blue eye
Was a glad listener, and the eager breath
Of pleased attention curled her parted lip.

And so I told her how the waters dried,
And the green branches waved, and the sweet buds
Came up in loveliness, and that meek dove
Went forth to build her nest, while thousand birds
Awoke their songs of praise, and the tired ark
Upon the breezy breast of Ararat
Reposed, and Noah with glad spirit reared
An altar to his God.

Since, many a time,
When to her rest, ere evening's earliest star,
That little one is laid, with earnest tone,
And pure cheek pressed to mine, she fondly says,
"Tell me the story of the Dove."

MRS. SIGOURNEY.

STORIES OF TIGERS.

e-nor′-mous	dan′-ger-ous	couched
jun′-gle	fort′-night	in′-stinct
o-ver-grown′	fright′-ful	with-drew′
slight′-est	deign′-ing	al-low′-ing
fail′-ure	lev′-elled	stealth′-i-ly
smoth′-ered	cap′-ture	Eu-ro-pe′-ans

In India there are enormous tracts of waste land, called *jungle*, overgrown with tall thick bushes and reeds. It is there chiefly that the tiger has his haunts. Every part of the world is full of life, and God has created the tiger for the jungle, till man come to clear and cultivate the land.

Have you ever thought of what use *whiskers* are to cats? Lions have great whiskers, and so have tigers, panthers, and all other animals of the cat tribe.

Wherever you find an animal with whiskers like the cat, you may be sure that that animal is meant to steal softly among branches and thick bushes. At the roots of the tiger's whiskers there are nerves, which make him sensible of the slightest touch. In this way he knows in a moment whether there is anything in his path which would make too much noise and alarm his prey as he creeps through the jungle.

The wild cat's whiskers were given her for a life in the woods; the lion's for the woody mountains in which he lives; and the tiger's for the tangled jungle.

In India, which may be called the kingdom of the tiger, he attains his greatest size and strength. He seizes his prey by day as well as by night; and when an army is marching near a jungle, it sometimes happens that a tiger will spring out with an enormous bound and a frightful roar, seize upon a man, and carry him off. Unlike the lion, he runs so swiftly that the fleetest horse cannot overtake him. By making bounds or springs, one after another, he clears a vast space of ground in a few moments. Should he miss his mark, he seldom renews his spring—at least for the time; he seems ashamed of his failure, and bounds off to his lair with a smothered roar.

Some years ago a number of English officers in India went out to hunt. In returning home after their day's sport, they found in the jungle a little tiger kitten, not more than a fortnight old. They took it with them, and when they reached their quarters, the little tiger was provided with a tiny dog-collar and chain, and attached to the pole of their tent, round which it played and gamboled to the delight of all who saw it. However, just as it was growing dark, about two hours after the capture, the people in the tent were checked in the midst of their mirth by a sound that caused the bravest heart amongst them to quail.

It was the roar of a tiger! In an instant the little kitten became every inch a tiger, and strained at its chain with all its baby strength, while it replied with a loud wail to the terrible voice outside. The company in the tent were panic-struck, there was something so sudden and so wild in the roar. Suddenly there leapt into the centre of the tent a huge tigress! Without deigning to notice a single man there, she caught her kitten by the neck. She snapped, by one jerk, the chain which bound it, and, turning to the tent door, dashed off at full speed. One cannot be sorry that not a gun was levelled at the brave mother as she bore her young one off in triumph.

When taken young the tiger seems capable of being tamed. The fakirs, a class of Indian priests who are in the habit of going about begging, often lead about with them tame tigers and leopards; but they are dangerous pets.

A story is told of a gentleman in India who nearly lost his life by a tame tiger which he had reared. He was sitting one evening outside his tent reading, with his pet couched down beside him. One hand hung by his side while the other held his book. The tiger began to lick his hand and continued to do so for some time. A low growl made the gentleman turn his head and look down. He saw that his hand was covered with blood. In an instant he knew that the fatal instinct of the animal had awoke, and that if he withdrew his hand, the tiger would at once spring upon him. Calling to his servant, whom he saw at a little distance, he told him to fetch a loaded gun and shoot the tiger dead on the spot. He then sat quite still, allowing him to growl and to lick the blood at his pleasure. We may feel sure the moments seemed very long to him. Speedily, however, the servant brought the gun, approached very stealthily so as not to disturb the animal, took a steady aim, and shot him through the heart.

The general way of hunting the tiger is with elephants. Though the horse can be made to face a lion, he will seldom face a tiger. The elephant, on the contrary, stands steadily while his rider takes aim just before the tiger makes his spring. The Hindoos rarely hunt or even fire on the tiger; they let him prowl about their houses, and carry away their cattle, and even their children: but wherever Europeans go, they strive to rid the country of such dangerous animals.

Sometimes in hunting, the tiger will spring out upon the elephant and fasten his teeth and claws in his neck or shoulder. Then the real struggle comes to be between the elephant and the tiger. The former will try to kneel on his enemy and crush him by the weight of his great legs and heavy body; but sometimes they both roll on the ground together, and a fearful combat ensues, generally, however, ending in the death of the tiger, either from the strength of the elephant or from a bullet from the hunter's rifle.

ELLIPTICAL EXERCISES.

nine	**gained**	**say**	**dish**
oaks	**seen**	**clinketh**	**never**
long	**gains**	**labour**	**late**

A penny saved is a penny . . . . . .
Better late than . . . . .
Better to live well than to live . . . .
Better to do well than . . . well.
It is never too . . . . to learn.
Idle people have the most . . . . . .
Little strokes fell great . . . .
No pains, no . . . . .
A stitch in time saves . . . .
Sin is sin though it be not . . . .
As the fool thinketh so the bell . . . .
Better small fish than an empty . . . .

THE ENGLISH GIRL AND HER AYAH.

at-tract´-ed	mor´-tal-ly	ad-ven´-ture
tim´-id-ly	strug´-gling	breath´-ing
hur´-ried	sense´-less	de-creased´
pur-suit´	Prov´-i-dence	be-thought´
veg-e-ta´-tion	re-cov´-ered	in´-no-cent
ter´-ri-fied	faith´-ful	mer´-ci-ful

A LITTLE English girl in India was one day playing outside her father's tent, near the edge of a jungle. Her attention was attracted by a beautiful little fawn, that seemed too young to run about, and which stood timidly gazing at the child with its soft dark eyes. The girl advanced towards it; but the fawn started back with a frightened look and fled. The child gave chase; but the fawn was soon hid among the tall reeds and grass of the jungle.

When the girl's ayah (nurse) missed her charge she quickly hurried after her. But so eager had the child been in pursuit of the fawn that she was some distance from the tents before the ayah overtook her. Catching up the girl in her arms, she attempted to return; but the vegetation around grew so high that she could scarcely see two yards before her. She walked some steps with the little girl in her arms, then stopped, and looked round with a frightened air. "We are lost!" cried the poor Hindoo, "lost in the dreadful jungle!" "Do not be so frightened, Motee," said the fair-haired English girl; "God can save us, and show us the way back." The little child could feel as the poor Hindoo could not, that even in that lonely jungle a great and loving Friend was beside her! Again the ayah tried to find her way; again she paused in alarm. What was that dreadful sound like a growl that startled her, and made her sink on her knees in terror, clasping the little girl all the closer in her arms? Both turned to gaze in the direction from which that dreadful sound had proceeded. What was their horror on beholding the striped head of a Bengal tiger above the waving grass! The ayah uttered a terrified scream, and the little girl a cry to God to save her. It seemed like the instant answer to that cry when the sharp report of a rifle rang through the thicket, quickly succeeded by a second, and the tiger, mortally wounded, lay rolling and struggling on the earth.

Edith, for that was the girl's name, saw nothing of what followed. Senseless with terror, she lay in the arms of her trembling ayah.

It was her father whom Providence had sent to the rescue. Lifting his little girl in his arms, he bore her back to the tent, leaving his servants, who had followed in his steps, to bring in the dead tiger. It was some time before the little girl recovered her senses, and then an attack of fever ensued.

Her mother nursed her with fondest care; and with scarcely less tenderness and love the faithful ayah tended the child. The poor Hindoo would have given her life to save that of her little charge.

On the third night after that terrible adventure in the woods came the crisis of the fever. The girl's mother, worn out by two sleepless nights, had been persuaded to go to rest and let Motee take her turn of watching beside the child. The tent was nearly dark—but one light burned within it—Edith lay in shadow—the ayah could not see her face—a terror came over the Hindoo—all was so still, she could not hear any breathing—could the child be dead! The ayah, during two anxious days, had prayed to all the false gods that she could think of to make Missee Edith well,—but the fever had not decreased. Now, in the silence of the night, poor Motee Ayah bethought her of the English girl's words in the jungle. Little Edith had said that the Lord could save them—and had He not saved from the jaws of the savage tiger? Could He not help them now? The Hindoo knelt beside the charpoy (pallet) on which lay the fair-haired child, put her brown palms together, bowed her head, and for the first time in her life breathed a prayer to the Christian's God: "Lord Jesus, save Missee Baba!"

"O Motee! Motee!" cried little Edith, starting up from her pillow with a cry of delight, and flinging her white arms round the neck of the astonished Hindoo, "the Lord has made you love Him! and O how I love you, Motee!—more than ever I did before!" The curly head nestled on the bosom of the ayah, and her dark skin was wet with the little child's tears of joy.

Edith a few minutes before had awaked refreshed from a long sleep, during which her fever had passed away. From that hour her recovery was speedy; and before many days were over the child was again sporting about in innocent glee. From that night the ayah never prayed to an idol again. She was now willing to listen to all that was told her of a great and merciful Lord. Of the skin of the tiger that had been slain a rug was made, which Edith called her praying-carpet. Upon this, morning and night, the English girl and her ayah knelt side by side, and offered up simple prayers to Him who had saved them from death.

A. L. O. E.

THE TRAVELLERS AND THE BEAR.

ob-served′	**trem′-bling**	**cow′-ard-ly**
at-tack′	**muz′-zle**	**de-ser′-tion**
thick′-et	**un-harmed′**	**whis′-pered**
squir′-rel	**some′-what**	**boast′-er**
pres′-ence	**a-shamed′**	**great′-est**

Two men were going through a forest.

"I am afraid," observed one, "that we may meet with wild beasts; I see the tracks of their paws on the ground."

"Fear nothing, friend Quickwit," cried the other, whose name was Braggart. "In case of an attack we will stand by one another like men. I have a strong arm, a stout heart, and—"

"Hark!" cried the first in alarm, as a low growl was heard from a thicket near. In an instant Braggart, who was light and nimble, climbed up a tree like a squirrel, leaving his friend, who was not so agile, to face the danger alone!

But Quickwit's presence of mind did not fail him. He could not fight, he could not fly; but he laid himself flat on the ground, and held his breath, so as to appear quite dead. Out of the thicket rushed a huge bear, and at once made up to poor Quickwit, while Braggart looked down trembling from his perch in the tree. One may guess what were the feelings of Quickwit when the bear snuffed all round him, coming so near that he could feel its warm breath when its muzzle was close to his ear! But Quickwit did not wince or move; and the bear, thinking him dead, plunged again into the thicket, leaving him quite unharmed!

When Braggart saw that the danger was over, he came down from the tree. Somewhat ashamed of his cowardly desertion of his friend, he tried to pass off the matter with a joke.

"Well, my friend Quickwit," he said, "what did the bear say to you, when he whispered into your ear?"

"He told me," replied Quickwit, "never again to trust a boaster like you!"

The hour of danger often shows that the greatest boasters are the greatest cowards. Let courage be proved by deeds, not words.

THE DUN COW.

an´-y-where	**high´-way-man**	**scram´-bling**
whisk´-ing	**vi´-cious**	**shrink´-ing**
dan-de-li´-ons	**caught**	**might´-i-ly**
saun´-tered	**wrenched**	**re-cov´-ered**

"YES, Mary, now that *I* am at home, you can walk anywhere with me, and fear nothing!" cried Marmaduke, whisking off the heads of the dandelions in the field with his cane, as he sauntered along with his sister. "If a highwayman were to attack us now, or two, or half a dozen, I would—"

"Oh, dear!" exclaimed Mary, suddenly, "I had forgotten that this is the field in which the farmer keeps that vicious dun cow! There she is!—she has caught sight of us!"

"Run! run for your life!" shouted Marmaduke, as with levelled horns, and tail in the air, the dun cow came rushing towards them!

Both the children began to fly at their utmost speed, making for a stile which was not far distant.

"Stop, brother—oh, stop!" cried poor Mary; "a bramble has caught my jacket! set me free—oh, set me free!"

The only answer which came was a bellow from the cow, which made Marmaduke run the faster, and alarmed Mary so that she wrenched away her jacket by main force, leaving half a yard of lace on the bramble!

Panting she reached the stile, and scramblin over in a moment, joined her brother on the sa side.

The ill-tempered cow gave another bellow, seein the children beyond reach of her horns.

"What does she mean by that roar!" crie Marmaduke, shrinking back at the sound. How ever valiant he might be against absent highway men, he was mightily afraid of a cow.

"I suspect," laughed Mary, who had recovere from her fright, "that her bellow means muc the same as the whisper of the bear to th traveller, in the fable,—'let courage be proved b deeds—not words!'"

A. L. O. E.

ELLIPTICAL EXERCISES.

tree	**fast**	**eats**	**climb**
keeps	**company**	**travel**	**die**
little	**noise**	**wheel**	**to-morrows**

Better to be alone than in bad . . . .
He who grasps too much holds . . . . . .
He that . . . . till he is sick must . . . . till he is well.
He that can . . . . . . well afoot . . . . . a good horse.
The worst . . . . . of the cart makes the most . . . . .
If you wish to have the fruit, you must learn to . . . . the . . . .
One to-day is worth two . . . .
Learn to live as you would wish to . . .

STORIES OF MONKEYS.

Gib-ral´-tar	sen´-ti-nels	chat´-ter-ing
cli´-mates	anx´-ious	fruit´-less
ven´-tur-ing	wool´-len	thiev´-ing
nim´-ble-ness	climb´-ing	snatched
sup-posed	a-maze´-ment	re-gained´
op´-po-site	un-u´-su-al	tri´-umph

MONKEYS are natives of warm climates only, and are found wild in most of the hotter regions of Asia and Africa; but in no part of Europe except about the rock of Gibraltar. There, in the clefts and crevices, they are frequently seen, sometimes venturing out and running along the heights with great nimbleness. They are supposed to have been brought thither at first from the opposite coast of Morocco, the nearest point of which is but a few miles off. Among the many amusing stories told of monkeys are the following:—

A sailor once went ashore on the coast of South America. He had with him a number of red woollen caps for sale. On his way to a town some distance from the coast, he had to pass through a forest in which troops of monkeys were everywhere seen climbing among the trees. At noon, as the sun was directly overhead, the sailor had to take shelter from its burning rays. He lay down to rest under the shade of a large tree. Taking one of the caps out of his bundle, he put it on his head, and, fatigued with his journey, he soon fell fast asleep. When he awoke, he found, to his utter amazement, that the caps were all gone! A most unusual chattering among the dense branches above him drew his attention. Looking up, he saw the trees alive with troops of monkeys, and on the head of each monkey was a red woollen cap! The little mimics had watched his proceedings, and having stolen his caps while he slept, had adorned their black pates with their booty. The monkeys gave no heed to his shouts, but kept the caps on their heads, and only grinned at his rage.

Finding every attempt to recover his caps fruitless, he pulled off the one which he had put on his head and threw it on the ground, exclaiming,

"Here, you little thieving rogues, if you *will* keep the rest, you may take this one too!"

No sooner had he done this, than to his great surprise the little animals instantly did the same. Each snatched the cap from his head and threw it on the ground! The sailor regained his property, and marched off in triumph.

A British officer relates, that being in India with the regiment to which he belonged, they had one evening after a long march encamped beside a forest. It was at a season and in a part of the country in which the nights are sometimes cold enough to render blankets needful. The men all slept very soundly; but in the morning several, whose tents were nearest to the forest, discovered that their blankets had been stolen during the night. The sentinels declared that they had seen no one go in or out of the camp. The missing blankets were anxiously sought for, and every place in the camp thoroughly searched, but without success. In the course of the day, however, the thieves were discovered. A number of monkeys were seen going about the woods with pieces of the stolen blankets round them, which they wore as shawls!

THE DAW IN BORROWED FEATHERS.

jack´daws	**pea´cocks**	**bor´rowed**
hap´pi-ly	**gath´er-ing**	**dis-ap-point´ed**
poul´try	**tur´keys**	**mis´er-a-ble**
al-lowed´	**pro-voked´**	**ri-dic´u-lous**

THERE were a number of jackdaws that lived very happily in the tower of an old church. Close at hand was a poultry-yard belonging to a large house, and among the poultry lived some peacocks, that were allowed to wander about the garden and in front of the house, that their beautiful feathers might be seen.

Now one of the jackdaws thought that there was

nothing he should like so much as to strut about, spreading his long tail in the sun, or drawing it up behind him in the shape of a wheel. And then, if he could shake all his feathers at once, and let them down as the peacocks did, while everybody gazed at him, he thought how proud and happy he should be.

So he resolved what he would do. He gathered up the peacocks' cast-off feathers, dressed himself in them, and began to strut about the poultry-yard in the hope of passing for a peacock! But he was quite mistaken: not only peacocks, but turkeys, Guinea-fowls, and even chickens and ducks, mocked him. And being provoked by his foolish vanity, they tore the borrowed feathers from him, pecked him, and drove him out of the yard.

The disappointed jackdaw then wished to return to his old companions in the church-tower, and would have been glad to lead his former happy life with them; but they would not notice him, and he was obliged to leave them, and lead a life of solitude and misery.

This fable is intended to show the folly of those who set their hearts on fine clothes, and who try to lead a life above their station. So long as they keep in the place which God has given them, they are happy, and people honour and respect them; but nothing is so ridiculous as the vanity which makes us try to seem finer or richer than we really are.

THE WONDERFUL PUDDING.

prom´ised	**ar-rived´**	**har´rowed**
ma-te´ri-als	**la´boured**	**quar´ried**
em-ployed´	**ploughed**	**wrapped**

OUR Uncle Robert came to us, and invited us to dinner. He promised to give us a pudding, the materials of which had employed more than a thousand men!

"A pudding that has taken a thousand men to make! then it must be as large as a church!"

"Well, my boys," said Uncle Robert, "to-morrow at dinner-time, you shall see it."

Scarcely had we taken our breakfast the next day, when we prepared to go to our uncle's house.

When we arrived there, we were surprised to see everything as calm and quiet as usual.

At last we sat down to table. The first course was removed—our eyes were eagerly fixed on the door—in came the pudding! It was a plum-pudding of the usual kind—not a bit larger.

"This is not the pudding that you promised us," said my brother.

"It is, indeed," said Uncle Robert.

"Oh, uncle! you do not mean to say that more than a thousand men have helped to make that little pudding?"

"Eat some of it first, my boy; and then take your slate and pencil, and help me to count the workmen," said Uncle Robert.

"Now," said Uncle Robert, "to make this pudding we must first have flour, and how many people must have laboured to procure it! The ground must have been ploughed, and sowed, and harrowed, and reaped. To make the plough, miners, smelters, and smiths, wood-cutters, sawyers, and carpenters, must have laboured. The leather of the harness for the horses had to be tanned and prepared for the harness-maker. Then, we have the builders of the mill, and the men who quarried the mill-stones and made the machine-work of the mill.

"Then think of the plums, the lemon-peel, the spices, the sugar;—all these come from distant countries, and to get them hither, ships, ship-builders, sail-makers, sailors, growers, merchants, and grocers, have been employed.

"Then we require eggs, milk, and suet."

"Oh, stop, stop, uncle!" cried I; "I am sure you have counted a thousand!"

"I have not reckoned all, my child. We must cook the pudding, and then we must reckon colliers who bring us coal, miners who dig for tin and iron for the sauce-pan. Then there is the linen of the cloth it was wrapped in. To make this we must reckon those who cultivate the flax, and gather it, and card it, and spin it, and weave it, and all the workmen to make the looms and machines."

Robert and I both said we were quite satisfied that there were more than a thousand men employed.

THE SALE OF THE PET LAMB.

sun′-shine	down′-cast	sor′-row-ful
pleas′-ant-ly	crea′-ture	pit′-e-ous-ly
nes′-tled	sub-dued′	im′-po-tent
la′-boured	mourn′-ful-ly	straight′-way
house′-hold	feign′-ings	through-out′

A THOUSAND flocks were on the hills, a thousand flocks and more,
Feeding in sunshine pleasantly: they were the rich man's store.
There was the while one little lamb beside a cottage door;

A little lamb that rested with the children 'neath the tree;

That ate, meek creature, from their hands, and
nestled to their knee;
That had a place within their hearts—one of the
family.

But want, even as an armed man, came down upon
their shed:
The father laboured all day long that his children
might be fed;
And, one by one, their household things were sold
to buy them bread.

That father, with a downcast eye, upon his thresh-
old stood;
Gaunt poverty each pleasant thought had in his
heart subdued.
"What is the creature's life to us?" said he;
"'twill buy us food.

"Ay, though the children weep all day, and with
down-drooping head
Each does his small task mournfully, the hungry
must be fed;
And that which has a price to bring must go to
buy us bread."

It went. Oh, parting has a pang the hardest
heart to wring;
But the tender soul of a little child with fervent
love doth cling,
With love that hath no feignings false, unto each
gentle thing.

Therefore most sorrowful it was those children small to see;
Most sorrowful to hear them plead for the lamb so piteously:
"Oh, mother dear, it loveth us; and what besides have we?"

"Let's take him to the broad green hill!" in his impotent despair,
Said one strong boy: "let's take him off, the hills are wide and fair;
I know a little hiding-place, and we will keep him there."

Oh, vain! They took the little lamb, and straightway tied him down;
With a strong cord they tied him fast, and o'er the common brown,
And o'er the hot and flinty roads, they took him to the town.

The little children through that day, and throughout all the morrow,
From everything about the house a mournful thought did borrow;
The very bread they had to eat was food unto their sorrow.

Oh, poverty is a weary thing; 'tis full of grief and pain;
It keepeth down the soul of man as with an iron chain;
It maketh even the little child with heavy sighs complain.

MARY HOWITT.

TAKE CARE OF THE MINUTES.

tire´some	walked	en-joyed´
min´utes	per´fect-ly	heart´i-ly
to-mor´row	shout´ed	e´ven-ing
whis´tling	quar´ter	prep-a-ra´tion

"I SHALL never find time to learn this tiresome lesson," said Robert to Frank as they left school; "I can't be ready with it to-morrow."

"You have ten minutes now before dinner; why not begin at once?" asked his brother.

"Ten minutes! that's nothing; besides, I must have a run with Rover now," replied Robert, whistling to his dog.

After dinner the two boys walked off to school again. Frank took out his book and began to learn. "What a book-worm!" laughed the other, and looked out for birds' nests in the hedge until they reached the school.

"Come off to cricket!" shouted a party of school-fellows as they broke up from lessons. Robert bounded away with the rest. Frank promised to follow in a quarter of an hour, and took out his book once more. Then he played away with the rest, and enjoyed the game heartily.

The boys were tired that evening, and went to bed early. But when they returned to school next day, Frank knew his lesson perfectly, while Robert pleaded that he had not had time to learn it.

"How did *you* find time, Frank?" inquired his master.

"I had ten minutes before dinner yesterday, sir, a quarter of an hour going back to school, and as much before cricket. Then I looked over my lesson before I went to bed, and took ten minutes before breakfast this morning to make it perfect."

"Which make an hour's preparation," replied his master. "Go to the bottom of the class, Robert, and learn that for those who take care of the minutes, the hours will take care of themselves."

ELLIPTICAL EXERCISES.

robbed	**spoken**	**undo**	**industrious**
boasted	**find**	**asked**	**majesty**
tied	**bade**	**work**	**stand**
			despair

ROYAL FAVOUR.

A FELLOW once . . . . that the King had . . . . . . to him; and being . . . . . what his . . . . had said, replied, "He . . . . me . . . . . out of the way."

REPROOF.

"I CANNOT . . . . bread for my family," said a lazy fellow.

"Nor I," replied an . . . . miller; "I am obliged to . . . . for it."

TOO FAST.

Two travellers were . . . . . . in a wood and . . . . to trees. One of them in . . . . exclaimed,—

"Oh, I am undone!"

"Are you," said the other joyfully; "then I wish you would . . . . me."

THE FLOWER NAME.

mus'-tard	ex-act'-ly	con-triv'-ance
grow'-ing	cor-rect'-ly	a-dapt'-ed
sprout'-ed	mil'-lions	con-struct'-ed
signed	in'-fi-nite-ly	pur'-pos-es
scat'-tered	fur'-nished	suf-fi'-cient

George. Mother, mother, come here! do come here! Look at this!

Mother. Well, my son, it is certainly very pretty; but I have often seen mustard growing.

George. But, mother, how did it come here?

Mother. How came these other plants here—these flowers and shrubs, of which the garden is full? The mustard grew here, of course.

George. But, no, mother, it could not have grown here by chance. Who ever knew such a thing as that to happen by chance?

Mother. What makes you think it could not have happened by chance?

George. Why, look at the little plants, how they have sprouted up so as to spell my name, G-E-O-R-G-E; not a letter wanting—not a letter in the wrong place.

Mother. Yes, it is spelled very well; much better, indeed, than the spelling of a little boy who once wrote a letter to his father and signed his name J-O-R-J-E.

George. Oh, mother, do not tease me any more about that blunder! But, indeed, I am sure chance could not have sown this mustard-seed. See how even and exact all the letters are at top and bottom. I am sure somebody did it, and I think, mother, you did it to surprise me.

Mother. You are right. I sowed the mustard-seed, but not exactly to surprise you. I did it to teach you something which I wish you to understand.

George. What do you wish me to learn, mother, from a bed of mustard?

Mother. You did not see me, a week ago, when I formed this little plot, where you find your name in these beautiful green letters,—how then came you to think that I had done it?

George. Oh, I knew that chance could not have shaped the letters so perfectly, and put them together so correctly;—I knew that some person must have done it.

Mother. And yet, all around us are millions and millions of things shaped more perfectly, and put together with infinitely greater skill.

George. What things? They must be very wonderful. Please show them to me.

Mother. Look, then, first at yourself. You have eyes most exactly contrived to enable you to see things around you. It would take hours to tell you of the wonders of the human eye. But without an ample supply of light all beautiful contrivances would be in vain, for light is required before we can see; and yonder, in the sky, millions and millions of miles off, shines a sun that gives just the kind of light to suit our wants.

You have also ears to hear sweet sounds and the voices of your friends. All the skill of man never made anything half so wonderful.

You have hands adapted to a thousand purposes, and than which nothing can be more wonderful.

Hours, and days, and weeks would not be sufficient to explain all the wonderful things about the human body.

If my dear boy thought that some one must have been at this bed of mustard, what should he think when he sees so many wonderful proofs of wisdom and goodness around him?

George. Oh, yes, mother, I understand, I see it all! I should be blind did I not see in all these things the work of ALMIGHTY GOD.

ELLIPTICAL EXERCISES.

Continued from page 48.

hear **here**	Standing . . . . ; do you . . . . what he says? Oh, yes; I . . . . very well.
hymn **him**	I heard . . . sing a beautiful . . . . and after a little I was able to sing it with . . .
hair **hare**	He caught a . . . . by a net made of horse . . . . in the field behind the wood.
know **no**	. . person that I . . . . will do it so well as yourself. I don't . . . . that. I have . . wish to do it.
lead **led**	They . . . him through the woods to the . . . . mines, and showed him how the . . . . was got.
might **mite**	Every . . . . of that cheese . . . . . have been removed before it was placed on the table. Yes, it . . . . .
neigh **nay**	. . . you are mistaken. I am quite sure you did not hear a horse . . . . . just now.
our **hour**	The . . . . is come when we must commence . . . work if we wish to keep . . . places in the class.
peace **piece**	Give each of these boys a . . . . . of the pie, and we shall soon have . . . . . among them.
prey **pray**	. . . . tell me how the lion and other animals of the cat tribe seize their . . . .
rain **reign** **rein**	Take the bridle . . . . into the stable from the . . . . or it wil be spoilt. Queen Victoria commenced her . . . . . in 1837.
rap **wrap**	. . . . up the parcel, and then . . . for James to take it at once to the post-office.
rote **wrote**	He . . . . . down the poetry so often that he could say it by . . . . though he did not understand it.
sea **see**	Do you . . . that large vessel far off on the . . . Yes, I . . . it, and a small one near it.
sow **sew**	Tell that girl to learn to . . . with a needle before she attempts to . . . onion seed.
sum **some**	. . . . persons think a hundred pounds a small . . . of money. I wish I had such a . . .

HOW A DOG GOT HIS DINNER.

cer´tain	hap´pened	im-me´di-ate-ly
be-long´ing	ring´ing	sat-is-fac´tion
re-ceive´	pau´pers	re-peat´ed
lib´er-al	reached	in-ge´ni-ous

In a town in the south of France twenty poor people were served with dinner at a certain hour every day. A dog belonging to the place was always present at this meal, to receive the scraps that were now and then thrown to him.

The guests, however, were poor and hungry, and of course not very liberal; so that the poor dog hardly did more than smell the feast of which he would have liked a share.

Now it happened that this dinner was served out to each individual as he came along, on his ringing a bell; but the person who served the dinner handed it through a small opening, and therefore did not see the person who received it.

Well, one day the dog had waited till all the paupers were gone; and having himself received very little to eat, he reached up, took hold of the rope by his teeth, and rang the bell. A good dinner was immediately handed out, and the dog ate it with great satisfaction.

This was repeated by the dog for several days; but the rogue was at length detected. It was thought, however, so ingenious and clever for a dog, that he was permitted to take his regular turn at the dinner; and thus he went on for a long time, ringing the bell, and taking his meal with the other beggars!

THE ANT AND THE CRICKET.

crick′-et	cup′-board	drip′-ping
ac-cus′-tomed	star-va′-tion	mouth′-ful
com-plain′	fam′-ine	bor′-row

A SILLY young cricket, accustomed to sing
Through the warm sunny months of gay summer
and spring,
Began to complain when he found that at home
His cupboard was empty, and winter was come.

Not a crumb to be found
On the snow-covered ground;
Not a flower could he see,
Not a leaf on a tree;—
"Oh, what will become," says the cricket, "of me?"

At last, by starvation and famine made bold,
All dripping with wet, and all trembling with cold,
Away he set off to a miserly ant,
To see if, to keep him alive, he would grant
Him shelter from rain,
And a mouthful of grain.
He wished only to borrow,
And repay it to-morrow:
If not, he must die of starvation and sorrow.

Says the ant to the cricket, "I'm your servant and friend;
But we ants never borrow, we ants never lend.
But tell me, dear sir, did you lay nothing by
When the weather was warm?"
Said the cricket, "Not I!
My heart was so light
That I sang day and night,
For all nature looked gay."

"You sang, sir, you say?
Go, then," says the ant, "and dance winter away."
Thus ending, he hastily opened the wicket,
And out of the door turned the poor little cricket.

Though this is a fable, the moral is good:—
If you live without work, you must go without food.

THE OSTRICH.

small´est	straight	dis-guised´
os´trich	doub´ling	ap-proach´es
height	fu´ri-ous-ly	poi´soned
ap-pear´ance	o-ver-pow´ered	val´ued
spread´ing	mis´sion-a-ry	Bo-he´mia
horse´back	feath´ers	con´quer-or

THE humming-bird is the smallest, and the ostrich the largest of birds. There are humming-birds no larger than bees, while the ostrich is often found ten feet in height, measuring from the crown of the head to the ground.

The home of the ostrich is in the sandy deserts

of Africa and Arabia. Among the Arabs it is called the *camel bird*, from the general appearance of its neck and body. Like the camel it lives in the desert, and can exist a long time without water.

Though the ostrich has wings, they are too small for it to fly with; but in running, it uses them like paddles. Spreading them out and flapping them in the air, it can run along at great speed. The swiftest horse cannot keep up with it! As described in the Bible, "*She lifteth up herself on high, she scorneth the horse and his rider.*"

The ostrich is often hunted on horseback, but so rapid is its flight that the hunters would seldom succeed in catching it, did they not know that it never runs in an even course, but zig-zag. So they let it go winding and doubling about, while they themselves push straight forward, thus saving time and keeping up with it. The pursuit sometimes lasts two or three days, till the poor bird is tired out; for though swift, it is not so strong as a horse. When taken, it will turn round upon its pursuers and attack them furiously, till it is overpowered.

Mr. Moffat, in his book called "*Missionary Labours in South Africa,*" describes the method of the wild Bushmen in hunting the ostrich:—A native is dressed with the skin and feathers of one of these birds, and thus disguised he approaches a flock of ostriches. He mimics the real bird, by pecking on the ground and shaking his feathers.

He trots and walks along until he gets within bow shot, when he discharges a poisoned arrow at one of the flock, and generally succeeds in taking his prey.

A traveller relates that at a French factory on the river Niger he once saw a young ostrich so tame that it allowed little black boy to mount on its back. No sooner did it feel the weight of the boy than it set off. At first it moved at a sharp trot, and then it stretched out its wings and ran with the fleetness of a race-horse round the village.

The ostrich is chiefly valued for the beautiful white feathers of its wings and tail. The young reader may not know that the crest of the Prince of Wales is formed of three ostrich feathers, with the motto *Ich dien*, meaning, "I serve." The origin of this is said to have been as follows: The King of Bohemia, who was slain at the battle of Cressy in the year 1346, wore this crest and motto. These were assumed by his conqueror, Edward, Prince of Wales, and have been worn ever since by the heir to the British crown.

THE UNFORTUNATE SPIDER.

re-sid´ed	con-sume´	cup´board
con-ve´ni-ent	for-get´ting	guess´ing
pro-vid´ed	pit´i-less	un-for´tu-nate
fa-tigues´	com-plet´ed	con-tin´ued
thor´ough-ly	cru´el-ly	pre-fer´ring

IN a little dark crack, half a yard from the ground,
An honest old spider resided:
So pleasant, and snug, and convenient 'twas found;
That his friends came to see it from many miles round;—
It seemed for his pleasure provided.

Of the cares, and fatigues, and distresses of life,
This spider was thoroughly tired;
So, leaving those scenes of contention and strife,
His children all settled, he came with his wife
To live in this cranny retired.

He thought that the little his wife would consume
'Twould be easy for him to provide her,
Forgetting he lived in a gentleman's room
Where came every morning a maid and a broom,
Those pitiless foes to a spider.

For when (as sometimes it would chance to befall)
Just when his neat web was completed,
Brush came the great broom down the side of the wall,
And perhaps carried with it web, spider, and all,
He thought himself cruelly treated.

One day, when their cupboard was empty and dry,
His wife (Mrs. Hairy-leg-Spinner)
Said to him, "Dear, go to the cobweb and try
If you can't find the leg or the wing of a fly,
As a bit of a relish for dinner."

Directly he went, his long search to resume,
For nothing he ever denied her,
Alas! little guessing his terrible doom;—
Just then came the gentleman into his room,
And saw the unfortunate spider.

So, while the poor fellow, in search of his pelf,
In the cobweb continued to linger,
The gentleman reached a long cane from the shelf,
For certain good reasons best known to himself
Preferring his stick to his finger.

Then presently poking him down to the floor,
Not stopping at all to consider,
With one horrid crush the whole business was o'er;
The poor little spider was heard of no more,
To the lasting distress of his widow.

JANE TAYLOR.

THE SWALLOW.

Af´-ri-ca	win´-dow	pecked
quick´-ly	eaves	hun´-dred
sev´-en-ty	through	swal´-lows
chim´-ney	spar´-row	pas´-sage

THERE are some kinds of birds that do not live in this country all the year round. When the winter comes they fly away to warmer lands, and return again only in the spring. The swallow is one of these birds; it spends the winter in Africa, and does not come to England until the month of March. It is a pleasant thing to see a flight of swallows at that time; for it makes us feel that the warm bright days of spring are close at hand. How quickly they sweep through the air, just showing their white breasts and dark glossy wings! Few birds fly so fast as they do. Their speed is said to be from seventy to eighty miles an hour. They seem never tired, but dart about, now here, and now there, after the insects on which they feed.

Some swallows are called *chimney* swallows, because they like to build their nests in chimneys There is another kind of swallow called the martin, or *window* swallow, which does not build in chimneys, but in the corners of windows, or under the eaves of houses. By the *eaves* of a house we mean that part of the roof which juts out over the wall. Here you may often find a martin's nest. It is not built of straw and moss, like the nests of other birds, but of little bits of clay, which the martin fits together just as we build a wall of bricks. It has a roof, and a little round hole to go in and out by; and it is lined with grass and feathers and soft tufts of wool. When these birds fly away to Africa, they do not forget the places in England where they have once built their nests. When they return in the following spring they are almost sure to come back to the same place, and to make use of the very same nest.

There is an amusing story told of two martins. One spring, on coming back to their old nest, they found a sparrow had already taken possession of it as her own. When the martins tried to get in, the sparrow pecked at them, and would not leave the nest. The martins called some of their companions to their aid; but, do what they would, they could not make the sparrow stir. At last they flew away, and the sparrow thought they had left her to enjoy the nest in quiet. But the next day they all came back. There were more than a hundred martins, and each had a bit of clay in its beak. Then they set to work, and walled up the door of the nest with the clay; so that the poor sparrow could not get out, and died of course from want of food and air!

There are many other kinds of birds besides swallows that leave us during the winter, for warmer countries. Others, that live in cold countries, come to England during the winter, and fly back to their own land when summer comes again. All these birds are called *birds of passage.*

ELLIPTICAL EXERCISES.

glitters	**needy**	**may**	**perform**
command	**quarrel**	**number**	**tongue**

It takes two to make a . . . .
All is not gold that . . . .
Be slow to promise, but quick to . . . .
A young man idle, an old man . . . . .
Do what you ought, come what . . .
Keep good company, and be one of the . . . . . .
Better to slip with the foot than with the . . . . . .
Command your temper, lest it . . . . you.

THE ROBIN'S PETITION.

sup′-pli-ant	**as-sent′-ing**	**con′-scious**
ad-mit′-tance	**feath′-ered**	**min′-strel**
pre-ferred′	**cher′-ished**	**myr′-i-ads**
house′-hold	**em-bold′-ened**	**scar′-let**
stom′-ach-er	**en-tan′-gled**	**flat′-ter-ers**

"A SUPPLIANT to your window comes,
Who trusts your faith and fears no guile
He claims admittance for your crumbs,
And reads his passport in your smile.

For cold and cheerless is the day,
And he has sought the hedges round;
No berry hangs upon the spray,
Nor worm nor ant-egg can be found.

Secure his suit will be preferred,
  No fears his slender feet deter;
For sacred is the household bird
  That wears the scarlet stomacher."

Lucy the prayer assenting heard,
  The feathered suppliant flew to her;
And fondly cherished was the bird
  That wears the scarlet stomacher.

Emboldened then, he'd fearless perch
  Her netting or her work among;
For crumbs among her drawings search,
  And add his music to her song;

And warbling on her snowy arm,
  Or half entangled in her hair,
Seemed conscious of the double charm
  Of freedom and protection there.

The migrant tribes are fled away
  To skies where insect myriads swarm;
They vanish with the summer day,
  Nor bide the bitter northern storm.

But still is this sweet minstrel heard,
  While lowers December dark and drear—
The social, cheerful, household bird,
  That wears the scarlet stomacher.

Then let us to the summer herd
  Of fortune's flatterers prefer
The friend like this, our winter bird,
  That wears the scarlet stomacher.

CHARLOTTE SMITH.

EFFECTS OF CARELESSNESS.

fas´tened	**re-mained´**	**dis-a´bled**
gen´er-al-ly	**wan´dered**	**pur-suit´**
con´se-quence	**i´ron-ing**	**scorched**
poul´try	**kitch´en**	**fort´night**
chick´ens	**daugh´ter**	**ac-count´**
re-mind´ing	**sprained**	**six´pen-ny**

THERE was a farmer who had a little gate which opened from his yard into a field. This little gate wanted a latch, and therefore could not be fastened.

When he passed through the gate he was always very careful to pull it after him; but other people were not always so mindful. Even with all his care, the wind would often blow it open again after he had closed it. The result was, that the gate was generally either flapping backward and forward in the wind, or standing wide open.

In consequence of this the poultry were always getting out, and the sheep and lambs always getting in; and it took up half the children's time to run after the chickens and drive them back into the yard, and to send the sheep and lambs back into the field.

His wife was always reminding him that he ought to get the latch mended; but he used to say that it would cost sixpence, and was not worth while; and that the children might as well be driving the sheep and poultry in and out of the yard and field as be doing nothing. So the gate remained without the latch.

One day a fat pig got out of its sty, and, pushing open the gate, ran into the field, and thence wandered into a large wood. The pig was soon missed, and a hue and cry was raised after it.

The farmer was in the act of tying up a horse in the stable; but he left it to run after the pig.

His wife was ironing some clothes in the kitchen, and she left her work to follow her husband.

The daughter was stirring some broth over the fire, and she left it to run after her mother.

The farmer's sons and his man joined in the chase after the pig; and away they all went, men and women, pell-mell, to the wood.

But the man, making more haste than good speed, sprained his ankle in jumping over a fence; and the farmer and his sons were obliged to give up the pursuit of the pig, to carry the man back to the house. The good woman and her daughter also returned to assist in binding up the injured limb.

When they returned they found that the broth had boiled over, and the dinner was spoiled; and that two shirts, which had been hanging to dry before the fire, were scorched and utterly ruined.

The farmer scolded his wife and the girl for being so careless as not to remove the shirts and the broth from the fire before they left the kitchen.

He then went to his stable, where he found that the horse, which he had left loose, had kicked a fine young colt, and had broken its leg. The servant was confined to the house for a fortnight by the hurt on his ankle.

Thus, without taking into account the pain the poor man suffered, the farmer lost two weeks' work from his servant, a fine colt, a fat pig, and his two best shirts, to say nothing of the loss of his dinner—all for the want of a sixpenny latch!

In this way were two good old proverbs verified:—

> For want of a nail the wheel comes off.
> Safe bind, safe find.

HALF THE PROFIT.

no´ble-man	**mar´riage**	**as-ton´ished**
re-sid´ed	**a-bun´dance**	**res´o-lute**
sea´shore	**fish´er-man**	**ac-cord´ing-ly**
cel´e-brate	**ap-pear´ance**	**dis-charge´**

A NOBLEMAN, who resided at a castle a long way from the sea-shore, was about to celebrate his marriage feast. There was abundance of meats, game, and fruits, for the important occasion, but no fish, as the sea had been very boisterous.

On the very morning of the feast, however, a poor fisherman made his appearance with a large turbot. Joy was in the castle, and the fisherman was brought with his prize into the saloon where the nobleman stood in the presence of his visitors.

"A fine fish," said the nobleman. "Fix your own price; you shall be paid at once. How much *do you* ask?"

"Not a penny, my lord; I will not take money. One hundred lashes on my bare back is the price of my fish. I will not abate one lash from the number."

The nobleman and his guests were not a little astonished, but the fisherman was resolute; they reasoned with him in vain. At length the nobleman exclaimed,—

"Well, well, this fellow has a strange whim, but the fish we must have. But lay on lightly, and let the price be paid in our presence."

After fifty lashes had been given, "Hold, hold!" exclaimed the fisherman; "I have a partner in this business, and it is right that he should receive his share."

"What! are there two such fools in the world?" exclaimed the nobleman. "Where is he to be found? Name him, and he shall be sent for instantly."

"You need not go far for him," said the fisherman; "you will find him at your own gate, in the shape of your own porter. He would not admit me until I promised that he should have half of whatever I should get for my turbot."

"Oh, oh," said the nobleman, "bring him up instantly; he shall certainly receive his half with the strictest justice!"

The porter was accordingly brought, and had to submit to his share of the bargain. He was then discharged from the nobleman's service, and the fisherman was amply rewarded.

THE COAT AND BUTTONS.

PART I.

ut'tered	fright'ened	shiv'er-ing
re-col-lect'	gam'bol	twist'ing
in-ter-rupt'ed	im-ag'ine	worst'ed
rough'ly	pit'e-ous-ly	stretched
shep'herd	at-tend'ing	jour'ney-men

"I THINK it would be very funny to hear my coat speak," said Edward one day. Scarcely had he uttered these words when he heard a soft voice from the bosom of his coat, which spoke as follows:—

"I recollect once growing on the back of a sheep."

Edward could not help starting back with surprise; but recovering himself, he said, "I am afraid, Mr. Coat, you do not know what you are talking about; for coats do not grow, nor do sheep wear coats."

"I was only wool when I grew on the sheep," replied the voice; "and a very pleasant life we led together, spending all the day in the green fields, and resting at night on the grass. Sometimes, indeed, the sheep rubbed himself so roughly against the trees and gates, that I was afraid of being torn off; and sometimes the birds came and picked off a few flakes of the wool to line their nests, and make them soft and warm for their young—but they took so little that I could easily spare it.

"We had long led this quiet life together, when

one day there was a great alarm. The shepherd and his dog drove all the sheep into a fold, and then took them out one by one and washed them in a stream of water which ran close by. The sheep on which I grew was sadly frightened when his turn came; and for my part I could not imagine what they were going to do with me, they rubbed and scrubbed me so much. But when it was over, I looked so very white, that I was quite vain of my beauty, and I thought we were now to return and frisk and gambol in the meadow, as we had done before. But, alas! the sheep and I were going to be parted for ever; and I was never more to behold the fresh grass on which I had rested with so much pleasure.

"Instead of setting the sheep at liberty, the shepherd took out a large pair of shears. Only imagine our terror!—the poor sheep, I believe, thought his head was going to be cut off, and began to bleat most piteously; but the shepherd, without attending to his cries, held him down and began cutting me off close to his skin. When the sheep found that the shears did not hurt him, he remained quiet: it was then my turn to be frightened. It is true that the shears did not hurt me either, because I could not feel; but then I could not bear the thought of being parted from my dear friend the sheep, for we had grown up together ever since he had been a little lamb. The sheep, who could feel, suffered even more than I did from the parting. As soon as he was set free he went about shivering with cold, bleating and moaning for the loss of his dear fleece.

"As for me, I was packed in a bag with a great many other fleeces, and sent to some mills, where there were a number of strange little things that were for ever twisting and turning round. They seized hold of us, and pulled us, and twisted us about in such a wonderful manner, that at last we were all drawn out into worsted threads, so unlike wool that I hardly knew myself again. It was still worse, when, some time afterwards, they plunged me into a large copper of dark dirty-looking water; but when I was taken out, instead of being white, I was of a bright blue colour, and looked very beautiful.

"Well, some time after this, I was sent to the cloth-mills, and my threads were stretched into a machine called a loom, and there I was woven into a piece of cloth. I was then folded up, and lay quiet for some time."

"Indeed," said Edward, "I think you wanted a little rest, after going through so many changes."

"Soon after," said the voice, "I was bought by a tailor, and lay on a shelf of his shop, when one day you and your papa came in and asked to see some cloth to make you a coat. I was taken down and unfolded on the counter with several other pieces, and, if you remember, you chose me on account of my beautiful colour."

"So I did," said Edward; "but you are not so *bright a blue* now as you were then."

"Something the worse for wear," replied the coat; "but if you stain me and cover me with dust, that is your fault, not mine. But to conclude my story: the tailor took out his large scissors, which made me think of the shears, and cut me into the shape of a coat. I was then sewed up by some journeymen, who sat cross-legged on a table; and, when I was finished, I was sent to you; and, ever since, I have covered the back of a little boy, instead of that of a sheep."

THE COAT AND BUTTONS.

PART II.

but´tons	**o´pen-ing**	**lathe**
jin´gling	**fi´e-ry**	**six´pence**
rub´bish	**so-ci´e-ty**	**showed**
stran´ger	**ham´mers**	**brushed**

Edward was much pleased with the story of the coat. "But these bright buttons," said he, "are not made of wool; have you nothing to say about them?"

"They were perfect strangers to me till they were sewed on," said the coat; "I know nothing about them; they must speak for themselves."

Upon this, the whole row of buttons raised their sharp voices at once, which sounded like the jingling of so many little bells. This made such a noise, that Edward could not hear a word they said. He therefore commanded silence; and, laying hold of one of them with his finger and thumb, he said, "Come, Mr. Button, let me hear the story from you, while all the rest remain quiet." Pleased to be chosen thus, the face of the button that was spoken to shone brighter than usual, and in a small, shrill, but distinct voice, he began :—

"We lay for a long time under ground, not bright and shining as you now see us, but mixed up with earth and rubbish. How long we remained there it is impossible for me to say; for, as it was always dark, there was no telling day from night, nor any means of counting weeks and years."

"But could not you hear the church clock strike?" said Edward; "that would have told you how time passed."

"Oh, no," replied the button; "though we had had ears, we could not have heard, so deep were we buried in the bowels of the earth."

"Oh, dear, how dismal that must have been!" said Edward.

"Not for us, who neither thought nor felt," replied the button. "Well, after having lain there for ages perhaps, all at once there was an opening made in the ground, and men came down where we lay, and dug us up. They talked about a fine vein of copper. 'I am glad we have reached it at last,' said they; 'it will repay us for all our labour.' They then put us into a basket, and we were taken up above ground, and into daylight. The glare of light was so strong to us, who had been so long *in utter darkness*, that, if we had had eyes, it would have almost blinded us. Well, after that, we were put into a fiery furnace."

"I am sure you must have been glad then that you could not feel," said Edward; "and were you burned to ashes?"

"Oh, no," replied the button; "copper is a metal, and metals will not burn: but we were melted; and, as the earth and rubbish which were mixed with us do not melt, we ran out through some holes that were made on purpose for us to escape from our dirty companions, who were not fit society for us. We were then shut up in moulds, where we were left to cool and become solid again. Men then came with hammers, and beat us till we became quite flat. Every time they struck us we cried out as loud as we could, and our cries were heard at a great distance; but they went on all the same."

"What!" said Edward; "had you voices to cry out?"

"No," replied the button; "but do you not know that if you strike against metal it rings or resounds? The sound of a bell is nothing but the metal tongue striking against the inside of the bell; and you know what a noise it makes." Just then the dinner bell began ringing, and Edward cried out, "That it does, indeed."

"Well," said the button, "after we had been beaten into flat sheets, we were sent to the turner's, who cut us into little bits, and then placed us, one after the other, into a strange kind of machine, called a lathe. He held us there while he turned a wheel with his foot so fast that it would have made one giddy—"

"That is, if you had had a head to be giddy," said Edward, laughing.

"When I was taken out of the lathe, I was quite surprised to see what a pretty round shape I had. I wondered what was to be done to me next; for as there was nothing by which I could be sewed on to a coat, I did not think that I was to be made into a button, but that I was meant for a piece of money."

"Yes; a round flat button is something like a sixpence," said Edward; "but then you were not made of silver."

"True; and I soon found that I was to be a button; for they fastened a tail to me, and rubbed me for a great length of time, till I became very bright. I was then stuck with the rest of us on a sheet of thick white paper."

"Oh, I remember," cried Edward; "you were all stuck on the paper when the tailor showed you to papa and me, and you looked quite beautiful." Edward then listened, thinking the button would go on with his story, but it was ended, and his voice was gone.

From this time Edward took more care of his coat than before; and when from any accident he soiled it, he brushed it clean; and now and then he was seen rubbing the buttons, to make them *shine bright.*

LITTLE ROBERT THE TRAPPER.

morn´ing	**dread´ful**	**ex-am´ine**
Eng´lish	**pick´axe**	**suf´fo-cat-ing**
Tues´day	**ac´ci-dent**	**gal´ler-ies**
miss´ing	**de-liv´er-ance**	**in´stant-ly**
res´cue	**fore´most**	**res´cu-ers**
star-va´tion	**fright´ened**	**grat´i-tude**

ONE morning while the pitmen were at work in a coal mine, they heard a noise louder than thunder. In a moment every lamp was out, and men and boys threw down their tools and ran.

It is Tuesday morning. The men reach the mouth of the pit, and count their number. Five are missing, four men and one little trapper,* Robert Lester. People above hear the noise and rush to the pit's mouth. The workmen are taken up. O the agony of the wives and mothers of those who are left behind! Brave men go back to their rescue. They light their lamps and reach the crush. There is nothing but a heap of ruins. Were the poor fellows instantly killed, or are they shut in to die of starvation? It is a dreadful thought. They called and shouted, but no answer. Up go pick-axes and shovels to clear the way. It is great labour and great risk. The news of the accident brings help from far and near. Men flock from all quarters to offer their services. How they

* The business of the trappers is to sit at the trap-doors which lead out of the passages of the mine, and to open and shut them as required. Often little boys are employed in this. It is not hard, but it is very dismal and tiresome work.

work! Towards night they hear something. Stop! hark! listen! It is not a voice, but a tapping. It can just be heard. *Clink, clink, clink, clink, clink!* five times, and then it stopped. Clink, clink, five times again, and then it stopped. Five more, and then a stop. What does it mean? One man guessed. There were five missing, and the five clinks showed all five were alive waiting for deliverance. A shout of joy went up in and above the pit.

Among the rescuers was the father of little Robert the trapper. Night and day he never left the mine, and hardly quitted work. "You'll kill yourself, Lester," said a fellow-workman. "Go take a little rest, and trust the work to us." "No, no, Tom," cried the poor father; "I promised Robert's mother we'd come up together, and so we will, if it please God," he said, wiping the tears from his rough cheek; and he hewed away with all his might.

How does it fare with the poor prisoners? They were frightened like the rest by that sudden and awful noise. Little Robert left his door and ran to the men, who well knew what it meant. Waiting till everything was quiet, they went forward to examine the passage-way Robert had left. It was blocked up. They tried another; that also was blocked up. Oh, fearful thought, they were *buried alive!* The men went back to the boy. "I want to go home; please, do let me go home," *said little Robert.* "Yes, yes, as soon as we find a way out, my little man," said Truman, in a kind yet husky voice. The air grew close and suffocating, and they took their oil-cans and food-bags to one of the galleries where it was better.

Truman and Logan were the names of two hewers. They were Christian men. "Well, James, what shall we do next?" asked Truman. "There is but one thing we can do," said Logan. "God says, 'Call upon me in the day of trouble; I will deliver thee.'" They told the boy of his danger. "But we must keep up a good heart," said the men; "and the way to do so is to put our trust in the Almighty God more than in man. He heard Jonah cry to Him from the whale's belly, and He can hear us from the bottom of a coal pit. Let us pray to Him." They all knelt down. Poor little Robert cried bitterly. But as the pitmen prayed, first one and then the other, their hearts grew lighter, and even the little trapper dried his tears.

When it was time for dinner they ate sparingly, in order to make the food they had last at least three days, for it might be that time before they could be dug out. Meanwhile what should they do for *water?* A trickling noise was heard. Water! water! Yes, it was water dripping from the rock. "It seems," said Logan, "as if this water were sent on purpose to put us in mind that God won't forsake us."

The men soon got their pick-axes; but what a hopeless task it seemed, to cut through the terrible mass of earth and stones to daylight! Their hearts beat with hope and joy when they first heard the sound of their friends working on the other side. It was then they made the *clink, clink* with their pick-axes, which was heard, and so encouraged their deliverers.

Wednesday, Thursday, Friday, and no rescue. What dark and dreadful days! Worse than all, the sounds beyond did not appear to draw nearer. And yet prayer and *songs of praise* might have been heard in that dismal cavern. By Friday morning their food was gone, and by Friday night their oil was used up. "Our food is gone, our light is gone, but our God is not gone," said Truman. "He says, 'I will never leave you, nor forsake you.' Can you trust Him still, mate? "Yes, I can," said his comrade. They tried to sing a hymn, but their strength gave way long before they got through. As for little Robert, he was so weak he could not sit up. His mind wandered, and he talked about the sun and the grass as if he saw them.

Saturday came. Five days, and the men outside knew there was not an instant to lose. They were too anxious even to speak. It was only work, work, work, for dear life. For hours they had heard no signals. Were their poor comrades *dead?* Suddenly the wall was pierced; a hole was made through; feeble voices were heard. "*Truman, are you there?*" "Yes, all here."—"*All living?*" "Yes, thank God, all living."—"All *living! all* living!" shouted the men; and the shout went up to the mouth of the pit. When Robert's father heard that his son was alive, the good news was too much for him, and he fell down senseless.

One hour more and the rescuers reached their comrades. Who can describe the meeting, or the joy and gratitude of wives, mothers, and friends, as one and another were brought up to the light? Here comes Mr. Lester with Robert in his arms! What a huzza rent the air as they came in sight. "Safe, safe! God be praised!"

MOTHER, WHAT IS DEATH?

laugh´ing	**case´ment**	**fu´ture**
pleas´ant-ly	**with´ered**	**light´ly**
daugh´ter	**chrys´a-lis**	**heav´en-ly**

"Mother, how still the baby lies!
  I cannot hear his breath;
I cannot see his laughing eyes;—
  They tell me this is death.

My little work I thought to bring,
  And sit down by his bed;
And pleasantly I tried to sing;—
  They hushed me—he is dead.

They say that he again will rise,
  More beautiful than now;
That God will bless him in the skies—
  O mother, tell me how."

"Daughter, do you remember, dear,
The cold, dark thing you brought,
And laid upon the casement here—
A withered worm you thought?

I told you that Almighty Power
Could break that withered shell,
And show you, in a future hour,
Something would please you well.

Look at the chrysalis, my love—
An empty shell it lies;
Now raise your wondering glance above,
To where yon insect flies!"

"O yes, mamma! how very gay
Its wings of starry gold!
And see! it lightly flies away
Beyond my gentle hold.

O mother, now I know full well,
If God that worm can change,
And draw it from its broken cell,
On golden wings to range,—

How beautiful will brother be,
When God shall give *him* wings,
Above this dying world to flee,
And live with heavenly things!"

ELLIPTICAL EXERCISES.

surprised	**candles**	**attacked**	**killed**
expected	**running**	**commodore**	**fight**
charged	**pockets**	**defended**	**vessel**
retired	**supplied**	**slept**	**magazine**

COOLNESS.

WHILE Commodore Anson's ship was engaged in close ..... with a Spanish ...... which he afterwards took, a sailor came .... to him and cried out,—

"Sir, our ship is on fire very near to the powder ...."

"Then," said the .... quietly, "run back and help to put it out."

THE SCOTCHMAN AND THE HIGHWAYMEN.

A SCOTCH pedestrian was once .... by three robbers. He .... himself with great courage, but was at last overpowered, and his .... rifled.

The robbers ...., from the resistance he had made, to find a rich booty, but were .... to discover that the whole treasure which the sturdy Scotchman had .... at the risk of his life was only a crooked sixpence!

"Why," said one of the rogues, "if he had had eighteen-pence, he would have ...... us all."

PAYING IN KIND.

AN eccentric old man once ..... at a hotel in a certain town. He was .... with two wax ...., which he did not use, as he .... very early to bed.

In the morning he found he was .... two shillings for wax candles; so, instead of fees to the waiter and the chamber-maid, he gave each of them a wax candle and walked gravely away.

ELLIPTICAL EXERCISES.

Continued from page 80.

steel steal	Did the thief . . . . . anything else but the watch and . . . . . hammer?
strait straight	We sailed . . . . across the . . . . . . of Dover to Calais in two hours.
time thyme	Your . . . . . looked very withered the last . . . . I saw it in the garden.
their there	I see that . . . . . is a wide difference between . . . . . opinion and yours.
throne thrown	When he had . . . . . . himself on his knees before the . . . . . . he begged for mercy.
too two	. . . spoonfuls will not be . . . much. Indeed, I would give him . . . more.
threw through	Frederick . . . . . the stone . . . . the window by accident.
wring ring	They may . . . . a bell for joy just now, but they will . . . . their hands for grief ere long.
weight wait	. . . . a little and he will tell you its exact . . . . . . I cannot . . . . just now; I'll come again.
weigh way	Stand out of his . . . till he . . . . . this sack. He will soon do it.
week weak	He felt very . . . . and fatigued all last . . . .; but he is better now.
wood would	. . . . . you like a walk in the . . . . before dinner? O yes, I . . . . . very much.
wade weighed	Did the soldiers, ... down with their arms and knapsacks, attempt to . . . . through the river?
won one	. . . of you has . . . the first prize, and the other the second.
your ewer	Where is the . . . . which I saw in . . . . room a short time since? It was a very pretty one.
yew ewe *you*	Did . . . see the . . . grazing beneath the . . . tree? No, I did not. When did . . . see it?

THE RUSSIAN SERF.

count´less	**sledge**	**whis´per-ing**
ap-proach´	**hard´ened**	**howl´ing**
Rus´si-an	**pol´ished**	**anx´ious**
no´ble-man	**sigh´ing**	**meas´ured**
trav´el-ling	**mean´ing**	**de-voured´**

In the dark forests of Russia, where the snow lies on the ground for at least eight months of the year, wolves roam about in countless troops; and it is a fearful thing for the traveller, especially if night overtakes him, to hear their famished howlings as they approach nearer and nearer to him.

A Russian nobleman with his wife and his only

daughter were travelling in a sledge, in the early part of winter, over one of the bleak plains of Russia. The driver was a serf, who had been born on the nobleman's estate, and who loved his master as he loved his own life. The sledge drove rapidly over the hardened snow, and there seemed no signs of danger. The moon began to shed her light, so that the road appeared like polished silver. At length the little girl said to her father, "What is that strange dull sound that I hear?" Her father replied, "Nothing but the wind sighing through the trees of the forest we have just passed." The child shut her eyes and was quiet; but in a few minutes afterwards, with a face pale with fear, she turned to her father and said, "Surely that is not the wind; I hear it again: do you not hear it too?—listen!" The nobleman listened, and far far away in the distance behind him, but distinct enough in the clear frosty air, he heard a sound of which he knew the meaning, though those who were with him did not.

Whispering to the serf, he said, "They are after us; get your musket and pistols ready; I will do the same; we may yet escape. Drive on! drive on!"

The man drove wildly on; but the mournful howling, which the child had first heard, began to come nearer and nearer, and it was perfectly clear to the nobleman that a pack of wolves had got scent and were in pursuit of them. Meanwhile he tried to calm the anxious fears of his wife and child

At last the baying of the wolves was distinctly heard, and he said to his servant, "They will soon be on us: single you out the leader, and fire; I will single out the next; and as soon as one falls the rest will stop to devour him: *that* will be some delay, at least."

By this time they could see the pack fast approaching with their long measured tread. A large dog-wolf was the leader. The nobleman and the serf singled out two, and they fell: the pack immediately turned on their fallen comrades and soon tore them to pieces. The taste of blood only made the others advance with more fury, and they were soon again baying at the sledge. Again the nobleman and his servant fired, and they shot two more, which were instantly devoured. But the next post-house was still far distant.

The nobleman then said to the servant, "Let one of the horses loose from the sledge, that we may gain a little more time." This was done, and the horse was left on the road: in a few minutes they heard the loud shrieks of the poor animal as the wolves tore him down. Again they urged on the sledge, but again their enemies were in full pursuit. Another horse was cut loose, and he soon shared the fate of his fellow.

At length the servant said to his master, "I have served you since I was a child, and I love you as I love my own life. It is clear to me that we cannot all reach the post-house alive. I leave my wife and children to you—you will be a father to them—you have been a father to me: when the wolves next reach us, I will jump down and do my best to stop them."

"No, no," cried the master; "we will live together, or die together." But the servant was resolute.

The sledge drives on as fast as the two remaining horses can drag it. The wolves are close on their track, and almost dash against the sledge. A sound is heard. It is the discharge of the servant's pistols as he leaps from his seat. Soon the gate of the post-house is reached, and the family are safe!

On the spot where the wolves pulled the devoted servant to pieces there now stands a large wooden cross, erected by the nobleman, with this text upon it,—"Greater love hath no man than this, that one lay down his life for his friend."

OLD FATHER WILLIAM.

heart´-y	**a-bused´**	**has´-ten-ing**
rea´-son	**health**	**cheer´-ful**
re-plied´	**pleas´-ures**	**con-verse´**
re-mem´-bered	**grieve**	**at-ten´-tion**

"You are old, Father William," the young man cried,
"*The few* locks which are left you are gray;

You are hale, Father William, a hearty old man;
  Now tell me the reason, I pray?"—
"In the days of my youth," Father William replied,
  "I remembered that youth would fly fast,
And abused not my health and my vigour at first,
  That I never might need them at last."

"You are old, Father William," the young man cried,
  "And pleasures with youth pass away,
And yet you lament not the days that are gone;
  Now tell me the reason, I pray?"—
"In the days of my youth," Father William replied,
  "I remembered that youth could not last;
I thought of the future, whatever I did,
  That I never might grieve for the past."

"You are old, Father William," the young man cried,
  "And life must be hastening away;
You are cheerful, and love to converse upon death;
  Now tell me the reason, I pray?"—
"I am cheerful, young man," Father William replied,
  "Let the cause thy attention engage:
In the days of my youth I remembered my God,
  And He hath not forgotten my age!"

SOUTHEY.

THE DUKE AND THE COW-BOY.

no´-ble-man	**dis-tress´**	**but´-ler**
gen´-tle-man	**sov´-er-eign**	**in-dig´-nant-ly**
res´-i-dence	**shil´-ling**	**sit-u-a´-tion**
man´-age	**ac-quaint´-ed**	**man´-li-ness**
know´-ing	**as-sem´-bled**	**hon´-es-ty**

ONE day a Scotch nobleman, who took a great interest in farming, had bought a cow from a gentleman in his neighbourhood. The cow was to be sent home the next morning. Early in the morning, as the duke was taking a walk, he saw a boy trying in vain to drive the cow to his residence. The cow was very unruly, and the poor boy could *not manage* her at all.

The boy, not knowing the duke, bawled out to him, "Hallo man! come here and help me with this beast." The duke walked slowly on, not seeming to notice the boy, who still kept calling for his help. At last, finding he could not get on with the cow, he cried out in distress, "Come here, man, and help me, and I'll give you half of whatever I get."

The duke went and lent a helping hand.

"And now," said the duke, as they trudged along after the cow, "how much do you think you will get for the job?"

"I don't know," said the boy; "but I am sure of something, for the folk up at the big house are good to everybody."

On coming to a lane near the house the duke slipped away from the boy, and entered by a different way. Calling a servant, he put a sovereign into his hand, saying, "Give that to the boy who brought the cow."

He then returned to the end of the lane where he had parted from the boy, so as to meet him on his way back.

"Well, how much did you get?" asked the duke.

"A shilling," said the boy; "and there's half of it to you."

"But surely you got more than a shilling?" said the duke.

"No," said the boy, "that is all I got; and I think it quite enough."

"I do not," said the duke; "there must be

some mistake; and as I am acquainted with the duke, if you return I think I'll see that you get more."

They went back. The duke rang the bell and ordered all the servants to be assembled.

"Now," said the duke to the boy, "point me out the person who gave you the shilling."

"It was that man there," said he, pointing to the butler.

The butler fell on his knees, confessed his fault, and begged to be forgiven; but the duke indignantly ordered him to give the boy the sovereign, and quit his service immediately. "You have lost," said the duke, "your money, your situation, and your character, by your deceitfulness: learn for the future that honesty is the best policy."

The boy now found out who it was that had helped him to drive the cow; and the duke was so pleased with the manliness and honesty of the boy that he sent him to school and provided for him at his own expense.

ELLIPTICAL EXERCISES.

reap	wealth	little
found	leap	danger

Look before you . . . .
Lost time is never . . . . . again.
Little . . . . . . little care.
Promise . . . . . . but do much.
Sow well, ... well.
Out of debt, out of . . . . . .

THE FOX AND THE STORK.

ma-li´cious	ap´pe-tite	has´tened
in-ten´tion	re-tired´	mor-ti-fi-ca´tion
prac´ti-cal	dis-pleased´	ad-mit´ted
ap-point´ed	com´pli-ment	gen´er-ous

A FOX asked a stork to dinner, with the malicious intention of playing a practical joke on his guest.

The stork came at the hour appointed, with a good appetite for her meal. But little pleased was she on finding that it consisted of mince served up in a dish so shallow that she could scarcely, with her long slender bill, pick up enough to satisfy a sparrow! The fox lapped up the food readily enough, only stopping a moment to say, "I hope, madam, that you relish your feast? Don't you think that my mince is first-rate?"

The stork made no reply, but retired hungry and much displeased from the almost untasted meal. A few days afterwards the stork returned the compliment by asking the fox to dinner.

Reynard hastened to the place of meeting, where the stork had made ready her meal. Great was the mortification of the fox to behold the food served up in a long-necked jar, which admitted the stork's slender bill, but into which he could not thrust even his pointed nose!

"I hope, sir, that you relish your feast?" said the stork, who was not generous enough to return good for evil, and who wished to give Reynard a lesson. And as the hungry fox looked sadly up into her face, she added, "Those who cannot take a joke in good part should never make one. Never do to others what you would not like them to do to yourself."

THE PRACTICAL JOKE.

re-luc´tant	**suc-ceed´ed**	**rhymes**
awk´ward	**in-con-sid´er-ate**	**re-lief´**
laughed	**cro´quet**	**ap-peal´**
an-noyed´	**ex-claimed´**	**in-hos-pi-tal´i-ty**

"But indeed—indeed I don't know how to shoot!" cried Anna, as Lydia forced her bow into the hand of her shy, reluctant guest.

"*Oh, nothing* is easier! you must try: just

put the arrow here, and place your right hand so—oh, how awkward you are!" laughed Lydia, as the arrow dropped on the ground.

"I never touched a bow before, I would rather not try!" pleaded poor Anna, who was really annoyed at making a display of her want of skill, before all the other guests at the Grange.

But the poor girl's annoyance afforded amusement to Lydia, who insisted upon her trying again. Anna this time, indeed, succeeded in sending the arrow about a dozen yards wide of the target; but her hand being unprovided with a guard, the recoil of the bow-string hurt her wrist, and the pain made her eyes fill with tears.

"I cannot—will not shoot again!" exclaimed Anna, throwing down the bow, and turning away from the spot with feelings of mortification which led to an evil desire to make Lydia bitterly repent her unkind, inconsiderate conduct.

About a week afterwards Lydia returned the visit. She was looking forward to a delightful day with Anna and her sister, and was full of glee when led to their play-room, especially as she spied a croquet-box in the corner.

"Shall we have a game?" cried Lydia; "croquet—or *archery?*" she added with a smile.

"Our games are of a different sort," replied Anna, going up to the table, on which were laid three pencils and some long slips of paper. "We are going to play at *terminations.*"

"Terminations! what are they?" cried Lydia.

"We have a set of words that rhyme together written on each of these slips," answered Anna; "see, here are *rat, fat, diversion* and *aversion.* Each of us will take one slip, and write a verse of poetry, each line ending with one of these very words."

"Poetry!" exclaimed poor Lydia, who could never even manage to compose a common note, and who was weak on the point of spelling! "I could not put two rhymes together, though my life depended upon it."

"Oh, but you must try!" insisted Anna; "you can't think how amusing the composing is! I daresay you will enjoy it," she added, with some malice, "as much as I enjoyed learning to shoot!"

To the great relief of Lydia, at this moment Anna's mother entered the room. "Oh, Mrs. Mayne," cried the girl, almost ready to cry, "must I write poetry to amuse Anna, whether I like it or not?"

"Poetry!" repeated the puzzled lady, turning to her daughter for an explanation.

Anna burst out laughing. "I am only acting out the fable of the fox and the stork!" she cried. "Lydia teased me with her bow and arrow, so I tease her with my pencil and paper."

"That fable," observed Mrs. Mayne, "was never intended to teach inhospitality to a guest, or petty revenge—as mean as it is unkind. Keep to its true moral, my child; which is, that since we find how painful anything like practical jokes are when played on ourselves, we should ever be care*ful not to* play them on others."

A. L. O. E.

THE DOG AND SHADOW.

re-flec´-tion	pos-sessed´	cov´-et-ous
car´-ry-ing	snatched	en-joyed´

A DOG, as he was crossing a brook with a bone in his mouth, saw his own reflection in the clear water, and took it for another dog carrying another bone. Not contented with what he himself possessed, the greedy creature snatched at the prize which he thought he saw below, and in doing so dropped the real bone, which fell into the brook and was lost!—The covetous, grasping at more than they have, often thus lose even that which they might in peace have enjoyed!

THE AMBITIOUS BOY.

shoul'der	**de-cis'ion**	**ea'ger-ly**
neph'ew	**ne-glect'ing**	**ir'ri-ta-ble**
bough	**an-nounced'**	**am-bi'tious**

"I NEVER knew before, Cæsar, that you were so fond of drawing," said Aunt Sophia, as she glanced over the shoulder of her nephew, who was busy with his pencil. "You really have made great progress."

"I need to do so," cried Cæsar, "if I am to carry off the prize for drawing, as I am resolved to do this term."

"I should have thought," observed the aunt, "that you had little chance against Lee. He is an artist's son, and has used the pencil, one might almost say, from his cradle."

"That will double the pleasure of beating him!" cried Cæsar, dashing the bough of a tree into his picture with an air of decision. "I'm working now at this four hours a day; he never draws more than two."

"You are not neglecting your Latin for it, I hope? You have had the Latin prize every term for these three years past," said Aunt Sophia.

"Yes," replied Cæsar, with a proud smile; "there is no boy in our class can match me in that, though Russell is now working hard. But I am not contented with *one* prize: I cannot rest till I have won the paint-box for drawing, of which Tom Lee makes so sure. It would be glorious to beat the son of an artist on his own ground!"

"Take care," said his aunt, gently laying her hand on his shoulder, "that you do not lose the Latin prize in trying for that which you are not likely to gain. Remember the fable of the dog that dropped the substance, catching at the shadow."

On the evening of the day on which the names of prize-winners had been announced, Cæsar came home from school gloomy and grave. His looks told his aunt enough to make her spare him the pain of questions; but his little sister Rosey was less observant, or less discreet.

"Oh, Cæsar!" she cried, running eagerly up to him, "tell me, are you to have the two prizes?"

"No," said Cæsar, with a growl.

"Only one," cried the child in a tone of disappointment.

"*Not one,*" muttered the boy. "I was so busy trying to beat Lee, that I could not hold my ground against Russell."

Cæsar flung himself on a chair, in so irritable a mood that even Rosey did not venture to question him further. Their aunt silently hoped that the lesson might prove worth the pain which it cost, and that the ambitious boy might not again require to be reminded of the dog in the fable.

A. L. O. E.

ELLIPTICAL EXERCISES.

answer	**salute**	**regiment**	**try**
returned	**allow**	**equal**	**manners**
present	**review**	**beat**	**exceed**

POLITENESS.

An English nobleman once .... the salute of a negro who was passing.

"Sir," said a gentleman who was ...., "do you condescend to ...... a slave?"

"Why, yes," replied the nobleman; "I cannot ..... a man in his condition to ...... me in good ...."

FREDERICK AND THE ENGLISH AMBASSADOR.

It is said that Frederick, King of Prussia, one day, at a ...... of a splendid .... of grenadiers, asked the English ambassador if he thought an ..... number of Englishmen could .... them.

"No," replied Lord Hyndford, "I cannot be so bold as say that; but I will ...... for it that half the number would ..."

PROVERBS.

sound	**fruits**	**fear**	**poverty**
employed	**enough**	**master**	**conquers**

A good servant makes a good ......
Better face a danger than be always in ....
Debt is the worst kind of ....
Deeds are ......, words are but leaves.
Empty vessels make most .....
Poor indeed is he who thinks he never has ......
The greatest conqueror is he who .... himself.
He is idle who might be better ....

THE ELEPHANT.

reach´ing	wrin´kles	Shef´field
four´teen	four´foot-ed	slaugh´ter
ma-jes´tic	vis´i-ble	as-sails´
ap-pear´ance	re-mark´a-ble	pierc´ing
hair´less	ob-tained´	po-ta´toes

THE elephant is the largest, strongest, and wisest of land animals. There are two kinds of elephants; the one found in Asia, the other in Africa; the first reaching the height of ten feet, the second that of fourteen. The elephant has, from his great size, a very majestic appearance; but otherwise he is no beauty. His huge head seems small when compared with the bulk of his body. His back is so long that many men might ride on him at once, if it were not at the same time too broad for them to stretch their legs across. His thick, hairless skin, usually of a dark-gray colour, looks like a covering of coarse leather, or the bark of an old tree, and hangs in wrinkles round him, as if it were too large for his body. "His legs," say the people of India, who take a pride in the four-footed giant, "are like pillars, his forehead is like a shield, his ears like fans, and his tail like a tremendous whip." The last, indeed, is more like a stiff rope, with a few thick hairs at the end. His foot is large, round, soft, and divided into four parts, having small hoofs overhung with skin so that they are scarcely visible. Yet, clumsy as he seems, the elephant sometimes runs so fast that a swift horse cannot escape from him! His neck is short and strong. His eyes are small and bright. But the most remarkable things about the elephant are his ivory tusks, and, above all, his wonderful trunk.

The tusks hang like swords from his mouth, one on each side. The male elephant has always a pair; the female sometimes none. These tusks supply *ivory*, which is employed for many purposes of use and of ornament. The tusks are usually from three to seven feet in length, but they have been found as long as fourteen feet; and they weigh from sixty to one hundred and sixty pounds. Ivory *is obtained* from the tusks of other animals besides the elephant, but those of the elephant furnish the chief supply. The demand for this article is so great, and the supply so constant, that it may seem a wonder that the noble race of animals which yields it has not long since become extinct. It is said that the slaughter of above twenty thousand elephants yearly would be required to meet the demand for ivory in the town of Sheffield alone! Many broken and shed tusks are found, however, in the forests of Asia and Africa; and then, in the north of Asia there are *ivory mines*, from which the tusks of thousands of elephants long since dead and buried are dug. The African tusks are the best, being harder and finer than those of India, and less apt to get yellow.

The elephant is commonly quiet and harmless, and a child may put a hundred of them to flight. When attacked or wounded, however, they turn with the utmost fury upon the person who assails them, and unless he has provided a way of escape, they seldom fail to catch and kill him, piercing him through with their tusks and trampling his body on the ground. The elephant, when tame, is exceedingly gentle, and does whatever he is bid. He understands the signs made to him by his driver, who sits upon his neck and guides him by an iron rod hooked at the end. He raises the knee to enable persons to mount; and with his trunk he even helps the person by whom he is loaded.

Wild elephants live and move together in large

herds. They feed upon grass, roots, and branches of trees; and love to bathe in a running stream. The tame elephant, as may be supposed from his size, is not easily kept in food. We have seen his bill of fare for one day, and it contained a bushel of barley-meal made into soup, thirty pounds of potatoes, and half a dozen pails of water, to say nothing of the hay and straw!

THE TRUNK OF THE ELEPHANT.

pro-vides′	ex-am′ple	breathes
va-ri′e-ty	de-sign′	length′ened
dif′fer-ent	re-quired′	in′stru-ment
pe-cul′iar	ad′mi-ra-bly	pro-dig′ious

God provides in a variety of ways for the wants and for the comforts of beasts, birds, fishes, and insects, as well as for those of man. And as the *end* for which He made them is very different from that for which He made us, He has given them bodies different from ours, and suited to their different ways of living and to the country and the climate in which they live. Every kind of creature has something peculiar to itself, fitted to lead us to admire the wisdom, power, and goodness of God.

The long trunk of the elephant is a wonder*ful example* of design and skill. The neck of four-footed animals is usually long, to enable them to reach their food without difficulty; but the elephant has a short neck, to enable him more easily to support the weight of his huge head and heavy tusks, the difficulty of getting food being admirably provided for by his long trunk.

The trunk of the elephant is to him what the *neck* is to other animals. It is also a *nose* to him, for at the end of it there is a hollow place like a cup, and in the bottom of the cup are two holes or nostrils, through which the animal smells and breathes. It is an *arm* and a *hand* too, with a very curious *finger* at the end of it, with which he feels, and does a thousand things easily and quickly. It has been said that the elephant *carries his nose in his hand;* and it might also have been said that he *breathes* by his hand. How strange it would seem to us if we were to breathe through our hand! At the extreme end of the trunk there is a curious part about five inches long which forms the finger. With this finger the animal can pick up a pin from the ground, or the smallest piece of money; he can select herbs and flowers, and take them one by one; he can untie knots; he can open and shut gates, by turning the keys or pushing back the bolts: and with this finger an elephant has been taught to make regular marks like letters, with an instrument as small as a pen!

The trunk of a full-grown elephant is about eight feet long. It can be made shorter or longer as the animal chooses, and can be moved with great ease in every possible direction. It has such prodigious strength that he can knock down a man with it, and can pull up trees of moderate size by the roots.

An Englishman who travelled a great deal in India, says: "I performed many long journeys upon an elephant, and whenever I wished to make a sketch, the docile creature would stand perfectly still till my drawing was finished. If at any time I wished ripe mango-fruit which was growing out of my reach, he would select the most fruitful branch, break it off, and offer it to me with his trunk. Sometimes I gave him some of the fruit for himself, and he would thank me by raising his trunk three times over his head, making a gentle murmuring noise as he did so. When branches of trees came in my way, he broke them off at once, twisting his trunk round them; but he often broke off a leafy bough for himself, and used it as a fan to keep off the flies, waving it to and fro with his trunk. When I was at breakfast in the morning, he always came to the tent door to be cheered by my praise and caresses, and to receive fruit and sugar-candy."

STORIES OF THE ELEPHANT.

Cey-lon′	en-gi-neer′	pre-tend′-ing
build	bal′-anc-ing	caught
bridg′-es	ob′-sta-cle	car-a-van′
church′-es	dif′-fi-cul-ty	loos′-ened
neat′-ness	sa-ga′-cious	wrapped
sat′-is-fied	tease	touched

IN the island of Ceylon there are large herds of wild elephants. Many have been caught and tamed, and have been made useful in helping to build bridges, houses, and churches. Travellers tell us that some of them are as careful about the neatness of their work as men could be. An elephant has been known to step back a few yards to see if it had laid a block of wood or stone straight; and then, if not satisfied, to return and push it into its right place. Some years ago an engineer in Ceylon had to lay pipes to convey water nearly two miles, over hills and through woods where there were no roads. To assist him in his work he had to employ several elephants, and nothing could be more interesting than to witness the way in which the elephant engineers did their work. Lifting up one of the heavy pieces of pipe, and balancing it on its trunk, each animal would march off with it, and convey it safely over every obstacle, to the place where it was to be laid. When it reached the spot, it would kneel down and place the pipe exactly where the driver wished. On one occasion an elephant, finding some difficulty in getting one of the pipes it had brought fitted into another, got up and went to the other end of the pipe, and putting its head against it, soon forced it into its right place.

In a show of wild beasts at Bath, some years ago, there was a large good-natured elephant. Among the crowd who went to see it was a baker. He thought it a clever thing to tease the elephant, by pretending to give it a cake, and then pulling away his hand. The elephant bore this for some time well enough, but at last got angry, and putting its trunk out of the cage, caught the baker round the waist, lifted him to the top of the caravan, [illegible] bumped his head with great force against the roof. Everybody thought the man would be killed. But all at once the elephant loosened its trunk and dropped him from the roof to the ground, in the very midst of the people. There he lay for a minute or two, looking half dead; but when the people came to him, he got up and walked away as if nothing had happened. He was terribly frightened, but not hurt. He never tried to play tricks with elephants again.

A person in the East, who often sat at the door of his house, near to a place where elephants were daily led to water, used sometimes to give one of them some fig-leaves, of which elephants are very fond. One day the man took it into his head to play the elephant a trick. He wrapped a stone round with fig-leaves, and said to the driver, "I will give him a stone to eat this time, and see how it will agree with him." The driver told him the elephant would not be so foolish as to swallow a stone. The man, however, held out the packet; but as soon as the elephant touched it with his trunk, he let it fall to the ground. "You see I was right," said the keeper, and went on his way. After the elephants were watered, the keeper was leading them back to the stable. The man who had played the elephant the trick was still sitting at his door. Before he was aware that the elephant meant to attack him, the animal ran at him, threw his trunk round his body, dashed him to the ground, and trampled him to death.

ac-cus´tomed	**hu´mour**	**wit´nessed**
treat´ment	**ap-pa´rent-ly**	**fa-tigued´**
re-ceive´	**drowned**	**car´riage**
ex-pect´ed	**pour´ing**	**care´ful-ly**

In the city of Delhi, in India, a tailor was in the habit of giving some fruit to an elephant that daily passed the place where he sat at work. So accustomed had the animal become to this treatment, that it regularly put its trunk in at the window to receive the expected gift. One day, however, the tailor, being out of humour, thrust his needle *into the* elephant's trunk, telling it to begone as he had nothing to give it. The elephant passed on, apparently unmoved; but on coming to a pool of dirty water near by, it filled its trunk and returned. Thrusting its huge head in at the window, it half drowned the poor tailor by pouring a flood of water over him, to the great amusement of those who witnessed the scene!

An army in India was marching up a hill. The large guns, which were very heavy, were drawn by elephants.

There was a long train of those animals in regular file, one close behind the other, each drawing its piece of artillery.

On the carriage of one of the guns, a little in front of a wheel, sat a soldier resting himself.

The man being very much fatigued dropped asleep, and in this condition fell from his seat.

The wheel of the carriage, loaded with its heavy gun, was just on the point of rolling over his body. There was no time to get out of the way.

The elephant in the rear, seeing the danger, but unable to reach the man with its trunk, seized the wheel, and lifting it up, passed it carefully over him, and set it down a little beyond!

A MONKEY ON BOARD SHIP.

pas´-sen-ger	con-ceal´	pen´-al-ty
mon´-keys	ex´-er-cise	touched
a-wak´-ened	jeal´-ous	an´-chor
pur-suit´	de-scend´	en-gaged´
ac´-tive-ly	pit´-e-ous-ly	ap-plied´
break´-fast	pun´-ish-ment	neigh´-bour-hood

THE following account of a Senegal monkey was written by a lady who was a passenger on board the ship in which it was brought to England :—

"We had several monkeys on board, but Jack, the cook's monkey, was the prince of them all. *Jack had* been first kept to his own part of the deck by means of a cord; but as he grew more tame he got more liberty, till at last he was allowed the whole range of the ship, except the captain's and passengers' cabin.

"At an early hour I was often awakened by the quick trampling of feet on the deck, and knew it arose from pursuit of Jack for some mischief he had been doing. He would snatch the caps off the sailors, steal their knives and tools, and if not very actively pursued, would sometimes throw them overboard.

"When breakfast was preparing, Jack would take a seat in a corner near the grate, and, when the cook's back was turned, would snatch up something from the fire, and conceal it. He sometimes burned his fingers by these tricks, which kept him quiet for a few days. But no sooner was the pain gone than the same thing was done again.

"Two days in each week the pigs which formed part of our live stock were allowed to run about the deck for exercise, and then Jack was happy as the day was long. Hiding himself behind a cask, he would suddenly spring upon the back of one of them, which then scampered round the deck in a fright. Sometimes Jack would get upset, and if saluted with a laugh from the sailors, he would put on a look of wonder, as much as to say, 'What can you have got to laugh at?'

"Besides Jack, we had on board three little monkeys with red skins and blue faces, and Jack would often get them all on his back at once, and carry them about the vessel. When, however, I began to pet these little creatures, he became jealous, and freed himself from two of them by throwing them into the sea!

"One of his drollest tricks was performed on the poor little monkey that was left. One day the men who had been painting left their paint and brushes on the upper deck. Jack enticed the little monkey to him; then seizing him with one hand, with the other he took the brush and covered him with white paint from head to foot! The laugh of the man at the helm called my attention to this; and as soon as Jack saw that he was discovered, he dropped his dripping brother, and scampered up to the main-top, where he stood with his nose between the bars looking at what was going on below. Jack was afraid to come down, and only after three days passed in his lofty place of refuge did hunger force him to descend. He chose the moment when I was sitting on deck, and swinging himself by a rope, he dropped suddenly into my lap, looking so piteously at me for pardon, that I not only forgave him myself, but saved him from further punishment. Soon after this I took another vessel, and Jack and I parted, never to meet again."

Among the rules of the port of London is one which forbids, under a heavy penalty, the firing of a gun from any vessel lying there. An armed *ship had* just come in from a long voyage, during which she had touched at several places, and at each of them on anchoring had fired a salute. A monkey that was on board, naturally wondering why this was omitted when he saw the anchor dropped at London, concluded that, rather than it should not take place, he would fire the salute himself! Accordingly, while the attention of all on board was engaged with the arrival of the ship, he went to the cooking-place, and with the tongs took out a live coal, which he applied to the touch-hole of one of the guns, and forthwith the whole neighbourhood was startled by the roar of the cannon. The captain of the vessel was prosecuted for breaking the law; and he could only clear himself by proving that the cannon had been fired by the monkey.

ELLIPTICAL EXERCISES.

enemies	**heaven**	**ditch**	**thoughts**
sown	**esteems**	**gathers**	**performance**

Much on earth, little in ......

False friends are worse than open ....

Promises may get friends, but it is .... that keeps them.

He that knows himself best .... himself least.

Many things grow in the garden that were never .... there.

Half a leap is a fall into the .....

A rolling stone .... no moss.

Give God the first and last of each day's ....

ELLIPTICAL EXERCISES.

condemned	sensible	pointed	destroy
notorious	destroying	judge	ordered
informed	offered	obeys	enforce
pointing	friends	reproached	officers
end	efforts	tried	enraged

THE KING AND HIS ENEMIES.

Some courtiers once .... a king, that, instead of .... his conquered foes, he admitted them to favour.

"Do I not," said the king, "effectually .... them when I make them my ....?

KING HENRY V. AND THE JUDGE.

When King Henry V. was Prince of Wales, one of his companions was brought before a judge for some crime.

Notwithstanding all the .... made in his favour, he was ....

The prince was so .... at the issue of the trial, that he struck the ..... on the bench.

The judge at once, with great spirit, ... the prince to be sent to prison.

Henry, by this time .... of the insult he had .... to the laws of his country, quietly suffered himself to be led away to jail by the .... of justice.

The king, Henry IV., was no sooner .... of what had taken place than he said, "Happy is the king who has a judge possessed of courage to .... the laws of his country; and still more happy to have a son who ..... them."

A SHARP QUESTION.

Jeffreys, a .... judge in the time of Charles I., ... with his cane to a man who was about to be ..... said—"There is a great rogue at the end of my cane."

The man .... at inquired, "At which ..., my Lord?"

THE SPEAKING CHIP.

char´coal	as-ton´ish-ment	re-ceiv´ing
ar´ti-cle	con-tempt´	set´tle-ment
su-per-in-tend´ing	ar-riv´ing	in-volved´
war´ri-or	re-solv´ing	mys´ter-y
in-ex-pres´si-ble	mys-te´ri-ous	sur-round´ed

As I had gone to work one morning without my square, I took up a chip, and with a piece of charcoal wrote upon it a request that Mrs. Williams would send me that article. I called a chief who was superintending his portion of the work, and said to him, "Friend, take this; go to our house, and give it to Mrs. Williams."

He was a singular-looking man. He had been a great warrior; but in one of the numerous battles he had fought he had lost an eye. Giving me an inexpressible look with the other, he said, "Take that! she will call me foolish and scold me, if I carry a chip to her."

"No," I replied, "she will not; take it and go immediately; I am in haste."

Perceiving me to be in earnest, he took it, and asked, "What must I say?"

I replied, "You have nothing to say; the chip will say all I wish."

With a look of astonishment and contempt he held up the piece of wood, and said, "How can this speak? Has this a mouth?"

I desired him to take it immediately, and not spend so much time in talking about it. On arriving at the house, he gave the chip to Mrs.

Williams, who read it, threw it away, and went to the tool-chest, whither the chief, resolving to see the result of this mysterious proceeding, followed her closely. On receiving the square from her, he said, "Stay, daughter; how do you know that this is what Mr. Williams wants?"

"Why," she replied, "did you not bring me a chip just now?"

"Yes," said the astonished warrior, "but I did not hear it say anything."

"If you did not, I did," was the reply, "for it made known to me what he wanted; and all you have to do is to return with it as quickly as possible."

With this the chief leaped out of the house; and catching up the mysterious piece of wood, he ran through the settlement with the chip in one hand and the square in the other, holding them up as high as his arms could reach, and shouting as he went, "See the wisdom of these English people; they can make chips talk!"

On giving me the square, he wished to know how it was possible thus to converse with persons at a distance. I gave him all the explanation in my power; but it was a circumstance involved in so much mystery, that he actually tied a string to the chip, hung it round his neck, and wore it for some time! During several following days we frequently saw him surrounded by a crowd, who listened with intense interest while he narrated the wonders which the chip had performed.

WILLIAMS' *Missionary Enterprize.*

TRAVELLERS' WONDERS.

PART I.

e´-ven-ing	**hard´-ened**	**un-pal´-a-ta-ble**
coaxed	**trans-pa´-rent**	**veg´-e-ta-bles**
in-hab´-i-tants	**dis-cov´-ered**	**va´-ri-ous-ly**
quad´-ru-ped	**ex-traor´-di-na-ry**	**pre-vailed´**
dwell´-ings	**pow´-dered**	**nau´-seous**

ONE winter evening, as Captain Compass was sitting by the fire with his children all around him, he began, after being coaxed a little, to tell them the following story:—

I was once, at this time of the year, in a country where the air was very cold, and the poor inhabitants had much ado to keep themselves from starving. They were clad partly in the skins of animals, and partly in garments made from the outer covering of a middle-sized quadruped, which they were so cruel as to cut off his back while he was alive.

They lived in dwellings which were partly sunk under ground. The materials were either stones or earth hardened by fire; and so violent in that country were the storms of wind and rain, that many of them covered their roofs all over with stones. The walls of their houses had holes to let in the light; but to prevent the cold air and rain from coming in, they were covered with a sort of transparent stone, made of melted sand or flints. As wood was rather scarce, I know not what they would have done for firing, had they not discovered in the bowels of the earth a very extraordinary kind of stone, which, when put among burning wood, caught fire and flamed like a torch.

Well—but their diet too was remarkable. Some of them ate fish that had been hung up in smoke till it was quite dry and hard; and along with it they ate either the roots of plants, or a sort of coarse black cake made of powdered seeds. These were the poorer class: the richer had a whiter kind of cake, which they were fond of daubing over with a greasy substance, the product of a certain large animal. This grease they used, too, in almost all their dishes; and when fresh it really was not unpalatable. They likewise devoured the flesh of many birds and beasts, when they could get it; and ate the leaves and other parts of a variety of vegetables growing in the country, some absolutely raw, others variously prepared by the aid of fire. Another great article of food was the curd of milk, pressed into a hard mass and salted. This had so rank a smell, that persons of weak stomachs often could not bear to come near it.

For drink, they made great use of water in which certain dry leaves had been steeped. These leaves, I was told, were brought from a great distanco. They had likewise a method of preparing a liquor from the seeds of a grass-like plant steeped in water, with the addition of a bitter herb, and then set to "work" or *ferment.* I was prevailed upon to taste it, and thought it at first nauseous *enough; but* in time I liked it pretty well.

TRAVELLERS' WONDERS.

PART II.

de-li´cious	**fi´bres**	**rel´ished**
tem´per-a-ture	**par-tic´u-lar-ly**	**ca-ressed´**
cen´tre	**man-u-fac´tured**	**ti´ni-est**
en-liv´ened	**dis-guis´ing**	**un-in-tel´li-gi-ble**
en-ter-tained´	**Hot´ten-tots**	**for´eign-er**
civ´il-ized	**stiff´ened**	**sa-lut´ing**

When I had sojourned in this cold climate about half a year, I found the same people enjoying a delicious temperature and a country full of beauty and verdure. The trees and shrubs were furnished with a great variety of fruits. These, with other vegetable products, made up a large part of the food of the inhabitants. I particularly relished certain berries growing in bunches, some white and some red, of a very pleasant sourish taste, and so transparent that one might have seen the seeds at their very centre. Here were whole fields full of extremely sweet-smelling flowers, that they told me were succeeded by pods bearing seeds that afforded good nourishment to man and beast. A great variety of birds enlivened the groves and woods. Among these I was highly entertained by one, that, with little teaching, spoke as plainly as a parrot.

The people were tolerably gentle and civilized, and possessed many of the arts of life. Their dress in warm weather was very various. Many were clad only in a thin cloth made of the long fibres of the stalk of a plant cultivated for the purpose: this they prepared by soaking in water, and then beating with large mallets. Others wore cloth woven from a sort of vegetable wool growing in pods upon bushes. But the most singular material was a fine glossy stuff, used chiefly by the richer classes, which, as I was credibly informed, is manufactured out of the webs of a certain kind of grub worm. This is a most wonderful circumstance, if we consider the immense number necessary to the production of so large a quantity of the stuff as I saw used.

This people are very peculiar in their dress, especially the women. Their clothing consists of a great number of articles impossible to be described, and strangely disguising the natural form of the body. In some instances they seem very cleanly; but in others the Hottentots can scarcely go beyond them. Their mode of dressing the hair is remarkable: it is all matted and stiffened with the fat of swine and other animals, mixed up with powders of various kinds and colours. Like many Indian nations, they use feathers in the headdress. One thing surprised me much: they bring up in their houses an animal of the tiger kind, with formidable teeth and claws, that is played with and caressed by the tiniest and most timid of their children!"

"I am sure I would not play with it," said Jack.

"Why, you might chance to get an ugly scratch *if you did,*" said the Captain.

"The language of this people seems very harsh and unintelligible to a foreigner; yet they talk to one another with great ease and quickness. One of the oddest customs is that which men use on saluting each other. Let the weather be what it will, they uncover their heads, and remain uncovered for some time, if they mean to be extremely respectful.

"Why, that is like pulling off our hats," said Jack.

"Ah, ha, papa!" cried Betsy, "I have found you out! You have been telling us of our own country, and what is done at home, all this while!"

"But," said Jack, "we don't burn stones, nor eat grease and powdered seeds, nor wear skins and webs, nor play with tigers."

"No?" said the Captain; "pray what are coals but stones; and is not butter grease; and corn, seeds; and leather, skins; and silk the web of a kind of caterpillar; and may we not as well call a cat an animal of the tiger kind, as a tiger an animal of the cat kind?"

BARBAULD.

TEA AND TALK.

fort′-night	**spoon′-fuls**	**emp′-tied**
dare′-say	**thou′-sand**	**tre-men′-dous**
hay′-stack	**build′-ing**	**wrin′-kled**
meas′-ures	**puz′-zles**	**cu-ri-os′-i-ty**

[*Matty making tea. Dick, Lubin, and Nelly round the table.*]

Lubin. One more spoonful, Matty; don't grudge the tea; you know that I like it very strong.

Matty. How fast the tea goes, to be sure! It is not a fortnight since I filled the caddy quite full.

Nelly. I sometimes think how curious it would be if we could count up all the pounds of tea that are used in England, Scotland, and Ireland, in the course of a single day. I daresay that if it were all piled up it would make a heap as big as —as a hay-stack.

Lubin. Oh, that is rather too much of a good thing, Nelly! You forget that every one measures out tea by tiny spoonfuls, and what a number it would take to make up the size of a hay-stack.

Dick. Don't laugh at Nelly, Master Lubin, till you are sure that she has not the right on her side. I happen to have been reading lately a good deal upon the subject. Tea comes from China in chests; each chest is about twenty-one inches high, and holds about ninety-six pounds of tea. Now, about two thousand four hundred and sixty-six chests of tea are used *every day* in the British Islands, and if they were all emptied out on the ground, I think that they would go some way towards building up a pretty high stack of tea.

Lubin. You don't mean to tell me that we drink up all that tea in one day!

Dick. You must remember that there are millions of tea-pots to be filled.

Matty. It puzzles my head to understand numbers. When one gets above a hundred, it seems all the same to me whether one talks of thousands or millions.

Lubin. That is just the way with me. I know how big a hay-stack looks, but I have not the smallest notion how many pounds of tea it would take to build up anything like it.

Dick. Suppose, then, that we measure by time. If the cart-loads of tea to be used in one day were brought to our yard, and we emptied out one of the heavy chests *every half minute*, it would take us—let me think—it would take us from four in the morning till past twelve at night to empty them all, even if we did not stop for a single minute to rest.

Lubin. Or to take our dinner!

Dick. It is said that *eighty-five millions and a half* of pounds of tea are used in one year in the British Islands.

Lubin. I told you that I could make nothing out of these tremendous numbers.

Dick. This may help you to understand them: If all the chests of tea consumed in a year were piled the one on the top of the other, they would form a column—[*he pauses to think*]—a column *two hundred and ninety-seven miles, five furlongs, forty-five yards, two feet and six inches high!*

Lubin. Why, that would reach to the moon!

[*The others burst out laughing.*]

Dick. Softly, my good friend. I cannot say that; but if laid on the ground it would more than measure the length of Scotland from north to south!

Matty. Oh, Dick! what a head for counting you have!

Lubin [*twisting a dry tea-leaf in his fingers*]. *I wonder* what the Chinese make their tea of.

Dick. You don't mean to say that you have never heard that?

Lubin. A little, dry, wrinkled, curled-up thing—it is like nothing else that one sees.

Matty. But all the world knows that it was once a green leaf growing on a plant.

Dick. A plant which bears white blossoms, something like those of our own wild rose. The leaves are gathered, three times in the year: the fresh young ones form the finest teas. As soon as they are gathered, the leaves are put into baskets, and then spread out to be dried, the finer kinds in the air, the coarser in heated iron pans. They are then gently rolled up with the hand, packed in chests, and sent abroad.

Nelly. It is strange that what comes from a distance of thousands of miles should be so common, that the poorest old woman would think herself badly off indeed if she could not have her cup of warm tea every morning and evening!

Dick. It was not always common. The Dutch are said to have been the first to bring tea into Europe. For a long time it was very costly and rare. In 1664 the East India Company made a present to King Charles the Second of two pounds of tea!

Matty. I hope that the Merry Monarch did not fall into the blunder of the old woman whose sailor son long ago brought her home some tea as a curiosity! She invited her neighbours to share the dainty, cooked the tea, *threw away the water in which she had boiled it*, chopped up the *tea-leaves*, and served them up with butter!

Lubin. Oh, what a dish! what a dish!—tea-leaves and butter! ha! ha! ha! what did her neighbours think of the treat?

Matty. They wondered that great folk should think so much of their tea.

Lubin. So she threw away the water! ha! ha!—that is not what I'll do, Matty, if you will pour out a good cupful now, with plenty of sugar and cream.

A. L. O. E.

SUGAR.

por´poise	**po-ta´toes**	**en-cour´aged**
ne´groes	**trop´i-cal**	**sub´sti-tute**
em-ployed´	**squeezed**	**clev´er-est**
con´ti-nent	**Ve-ne´ti-an**	**ep´i-gram**
pos-ses´sions	**thir´teenth**	**sweet´meats**

[*Dick, Lubin, Matty, and Nelly, at breakfast.*]

Dick. Hollo! stop Master Lubin; put down these sugar-tongs, if you please. You have had four lumps of sugar already, and if you go on at that rate you will grow as fat as a little porpoise!

Lubin. Why should I grow so fat?

Dick. Because it is the property of sugar to fatten. It is said that the negroes, when employed in cutting sugar-canes, live entirely on the produce *for the time*, and grow quite plump on the sweets!

Nelly. I suppose that in the British Islands we use as much sugar as tea.

Dick. More; a great deal more.

Matty. Think of all the sugar used in preserves—

Lubin. Tarts, puddings, jellies, and hundreds of other things.

Dick. It is said that we consume sugar at the rate of thirty-seven pounds weight a head during the year; but I am sure, my good Lubin, that you have a hundred-weight at least for your share.

Nelly. What a quantity must be eaten in England, Scotland, Ireland, and Wales!

Dick. Enough, if packed in tea-chests, to make a row *thirteen hundred and eighty-five miles long.* That would nearly reach from Ireland to Newfoundland across the great Atlantic!

Nelly. Where does all the sugar come from?

Dick. A great deal comes from the West Indies, some from the continent of America, some from our own possessions in India.

Lubin. Can we not grow it here? I should like a field of sugar-canes much better than a field of potatoes.

Dick. I daresay you would, my fine fellow; but the cane requires a great deal more heat than we ever have in Old England. Only black men seem to be able to endure the fatigue of hoeing the plantations under a burning tropical sun.

Matty. What is the sugar-cane like?

Dick. It is something like a gigantic reed, with a jointed stem, twelve or fourteen feet in height,

bearing on the top a graceful drooping tuft of flowers;—that is to say, it would do so if the cane were not cut down before the flowers had time to form. These canes are carried to a mill, where all their sweet juice is crushed out.

Lubin. There is some treacle on the table; is that squeezed out of a cane?

Dick. That is the liquid which drains from the sugar, the part which will not harden into grains like the brown sugar there in the cupboard.

Lubin. And how comes this loaf-sugar to be so white? [*He drops a fifth lump into his tea.*]

Dick. It is carefully cleared and refined.

Nelly. And when did sugar first come to Europe?

Dick. I have heard that it was brought over by Marco Polo, a famous Venetian traveller, in the middle of the thirteenth century; but sugar had been known to the Chinese nation for two thousand years before that.

Lubin. And so those funny fellows with their hair in long tails were feasting on all kinds of sweets when our poor forefathers—

Dick. Were eating berries and acorns!

Lubin. Ah, well, we shall make up for lost time now. [*He drops a sixth lump into his tea. Matty, laughing, puts the sugar basin out of his reach.*]

Nelly. Can sugar be got from nothing but canes?

Dick. O yes; many plants contain sugar, but few in sufficient quantity to make it worth our while to cultivate them for the purpose. The maple has been used in America; and in France the beet-root has been tried.

Matty. What! that vegetable that is of such a lovely bright red, that I often wish I could dye my bonnet ribbons with the juice?

Dick. That's it, Matty; that is what has been cultivated for the sake of the sugar that it yields. Napoleon Buonaparte at one time encouraged the growth of beet-root, in the hope of ruining our West Indian plantations by providing a substitute for their canes.

Nelly. What is a *substitute,* Dick?

Dick. Something that will take the place of another thing.

Matty. And did Napoleon's plan produce much sugar?

Dick. I do not know about that; I only know that it was the cause of the production of one of the cleverest epigrams that ever was written, faulty though it may be in spelling and grammar.

Lubin. Give us the epigram, Dick, if it is anything funny or merry.

Dick.—

"Says Bony, 'I now have a substitute found,
And no longer require your sweet.'
'Very well,' says John Bull, 'I will then *use the cane,*
Since you are content to get *beet.*'"

[*All the children laugh except Lubin, who rubs his head as he cannot make out the joke.*]

Nelly. But now that the French and we are allies—

Dick. They will help to buy our cane sugar in a friendly way; and in a friendly way we will help to eat up their sweetmeats. Matty, just hand in your box of bon-bons!

A. L. O. E.

SONG OF THE GRASS.

creep´ing	**cheer´ing**	**num´bered**
ev´er-y-where	**toil´ing**	**nar´row**
sha´dy	**si´lent-ly**	**grate´ful-ly**
noi´sy	**qui´et-ly**	**beau´ti-fy**

HERE I come, creeping, creeping everywhere;
By the dusty road-side,
On the sunny hill-side,
Close by the noisy brook,
In ev'ry shady nook,
I come, creeping, creeping everywhere.

In the noisy city street
My pleasant face you'll meet
Cheering the sick at heart,
Toiling his busy part,
Silently creeping, creeping everywhere.

You cannot see me coming,
Nor hear my low, sweet humming;
For in the starry night,
And the glad morning light,
I come, quietly creeping everywhere.

When you're numbered with the dead
In your still and narrow bed,
In the happy Spring I'll come
And deck your silent home,
Creeping, silently creeping everywhere.

My humble song of praise
Most gratefully I raise
To Him at whose command
I beautify the land;
Creeping, silently creeping everywhere.

KINDNESS TO ANIMALS.

help´less	re-quired´	crea´tures
way´ward	bound´less	re-ceive´
de-ride´	be-stowed´	light´ly

TURN, turn thy hasty foot aside,
Nor crush that helpless worm;
The frame thy wayward looks deride
Required a God to form.

The common Lord of all that move,
From whom thy being flowed,
A portion of His boundless love
On that poor worm bestowed.

The sun, the moon, the stars He made,
To all His creatures free;
And spreads o'er earth the grassy blade
For worms as well as thee.

Let them enjoy their little day,
Their lowly bliss receive;—
O do not lightly take away
The life thou canst not give.

GISBORN.

DON'T BE TOO SURE.

Na-po´-le-on	in-va´-sion	Wel´-ling-ton
Buo´-na-parte	in-ter-rupt´-ed	Por´-tu-gal
con´-quest	con-tin´-ued	Por-tu-guese´
chan´-nel	a-shamed´	in-vin´-ci-ble
cel´-e-brate	Wa-ter-loo´	un-der-neath´

"FATHER, don't you want me to be clever and great?" said Willie to his father one day.

"I want you, my boy, to do your duty in the station, whatever it may be, to which it shall please God to call you, and not to set your heart on, or make too sure of, any mere earthly success. When I see folk, as the saying goes, counting their chickens before they are hatched, it brings into my mind what I read lately about the famous Napoleon Buonaparte."

"Oh, let me hear about him, father. You can talk quite well at your work, and I like to hear what you get out of those learned books that you read."

"This was taken out of a large work, written by an Earl, the Life of the great William Pitt," said the father; "and it is all true—I have not a doubt of it. When Buonaparte was ruling over France, he wished to rule over old England too; and so, being sure of conquest, he fixed on the very time when he would come over and invade us. He got a number of his soldiers together, and had ships to carry them across, and he looked over the blue waves of the Channel, and thinks he, 'I'll soon land in England, march up to London and take it."

"He made too sure," laughed Willie.

"He made *so* sure," said the father, "that—would you believe it, my boy?—he had actually *a medal made to celebrate his invasion of England!*"

"But he never invaded it!" interrupted Willie.

"And on the medal was stamped in French, '*Struck at London,*'" continued the father.

"But he never entered London!" cried Willie.

"He made *so sure* of success," said the father, "that he prepared a medal in honour of the conquest of a city that he was never so much as to set his foot in!"

"Well, that was counting his chickens before they were hatched—making too sure!" exclaimed the boy. "How ashamed Buonaparte must afterwards have felt, whenever he thought of that medal!—Have you any more stories for me, father?"

"Yes; I remember another, which I read some time ago," replied the father. "It's about a very different man from him who struck the medal;—it's about the Duke of Wellington—"

"Who beat Napoleon Buonaparte himself at the battle of Waterloo!" cried Willie. "I hope that *he* hadn't his medal ready beforehand?"

"You know, or perhaps you don't know, my lad, that Wellington was sent over to Portugal to help the poor folk there who were fighting against the French. God gave wisdom to our great general, and success to a good cause, so the enemy's soldiers were driven out, and Portugal was free!"

"How glad the Portuguese must have been," cried Willie; "and how they must have honoured our Duke! That was the time for striking a medal—when the battle had been fought and won."

"I don't know whether a medal was struck," said the father; "but I'll tell you what the Portuguese did. They had a print made of the general, and under it were these words in Latin, '*Invincible Wellington, from grateful Portugal.*'"

"What does 'invincible' mean, father?"

"It means—one who cannot be conquered."

"Oh, that was making *too sure!* The Duke might have won a hundred victories, but as long as he lived no one could tell that he might not be beaten at last."

"Just hear the end of my story, my boy, and you'll see that the Duke was quite of your mind in that matter. A friend asked him to send him the print; so Wellington got a copy and sent it. But he would not allow that boasting word to be at the bottom of his likeness, as if he thought himself sure of victory. He scored out '*invincible*' with a dash of his pen, and underneath it he wrote, 'Don't halloo till you are out of the wood."

Willie burst out laughing. "That showed the Duke's good sense," said he.

"Ay, and good feeling too, my boy. It showed that he was not a man of a boastful spirit, but knew that the highest may have a fall. When you are tempted, Willie, to make too sure of the morrow, just think of Buonaparte and his medal—of Wellington and his print."

A. L. O. E.

THE TWO RULES, AND HOW THEY WORKED.

fa´vour-ite	vex-a´tious	mis´chief
in-quired´	wor´ried	an´swered
ob-jec´tion	op-por-tu´ni-ties	sup-press´
our-selves´	val´u-a-ble	em-broi´der-y
pro-posed´	to-mor´row	sen´si-ble

"HERE are two rules for you, Fred," said Giles Warner, looking up from the paper he was reading and speaking to a younger brother, who was sitting by the fire playing with a favourite dog.

"Well, what are they?" said Fred, stopping his sport with his dog.

"The first is, '*Never get vexed with anything you can help.*' The second is, '*Never get vexed with anything you can't help.*'"

"Cannot these rules be as useful to you as to me?" inquired Fred, archly.

"No doubt of that," replied Giles; "but what say you, if we both should adopt them?"

"*I think* they take a pretty wide sweep," said

Fred. "They leave one no chance at all to get vexed."

"That might be an objection to them," said Giles, "if any one were wiser, better, or happier for getting vexed. I think they are sensible rules. It is *foolish* to vex ourselves about anything that can be helped, and it is *useless* to vex ourselves about what can't be helped. Let us help each other to remember and obey these two simple rules. What say you?"

"I'll agree to it," said Fred, who was usually ready to agree to anything his brother proposed, if it was only proposed pleasantly.

"That's too bad!" exclaimed Fred the next morning, while preparing for school.

"What is the matter?" inquired Giles.

"I have broken my shoe-string, and it is vexatious; I am in such a hurry."

"It is vexatious, no doubt," replied Giles, "but you must not get vexed; for this is one of the things that *can* be helped. You can find a string in the left drawer in my room."

"But we shall be late at school," said Fred.

"No, no," said Giles. "We shall only have to walk a little faster. Besides, if you keep cool, you will find the string, and put it in, much sooner than if you become vexed and worried."

"That's true," said Fred, as he started for the string, quite restored to good humour.

Several opportunities occurred during the day for putting into practice the newly adopted rules. *The last was this:—*

In the evening, Giles broke the blade of his knife, while cutting a hard piece of wood.

"It can't be helped," said Fred, "so you must not get vexed about it."

"It might have been helped," said Giles, "but I can do better than to fret about it. I can learn a lesson of care for the future, which may some day save a knife more valuable than this. These rules work well. Let us try them again to-morrow."

The next morning Fred devoted an hour before school to writing. After he had written half a dozen lines, his mother called him away to do something for her. During his absence, his sister Lucy made use of his pen and ink to write her name in a school-book. In doing this, she let fall a drop of ink on the page he had been writing. Fred returned while she was busily employed in doing what she could to repair the mischief.

"You have made a great blot on my copy-book," he exclaimed, looking over her shoulder.

"I am very sorry. I did not mean to do it," said Lucy.

Fred was so vexed, that he would have answered his sister very roughly, if Giles had not been there.

"Take care, Fred; you know the thing is done, and can't be helped."

Fred tried hard to suppress his vexation. "I know it was an accident," he said pleasantly, after a brief struggle with himself.

Lucy left the room, and Fred sat down again

to write. After a moment, he looked up. "No great harm has been done, after all," he said. "Two or three alterations are much needed, and, if I write my copy over again, I can make them."

"So much for not getting vexed," said Giles, laughing. "Our rules work well."

At night Fred tore his coat while climbing over a fence.

"That's too bad," said he.

"It can't be helped," said Giles; "it can be mended."

"Yes, but that's what troubles me," said Fred. "I don't like to ask mother to mend it, she has so much to do."

Giles proposed that Fred should ask Lucy to do it for him, as her mother had taught her to mend very neatly. Fred was at first not disposed to adopt this measure. He knew that Lucy very much disliked mending, and was afràid she should be cross if asked to do it; but he at last decided to run the risk of that. They found Lucy busily employed with a piece of embroidery, and quite absorbed with her work. Fred looked at Giles when he saw how his sister was occupied; but he had gone too far to retreat.

"I wish to ask a great favour of you, Lucy," said Fred; "but I fear I have come at a wrong time."

"What do you want?" said Lucy.

"I am almost afraid to tell you. It is too bad to ask you to leave that pretty work to do what you dislike."

"You are a long while in telling me what is wanted," said Lucy, laughing. "Come, out with it."

Fred, thus encouraged, held up his arm and displayed the rent.

"Well, well, take it off, and I will do my best," said Lucy, cheerfully.

"You are a dear, good sister," said Fred. "When I saw what you were about, I thought that you would not be willing to do it."

"My good nature quite puzzles you, does it?" said Lucy, laughing. "I shall have to let you into a secret. To tell the truth, I have been thinking all day what I could do for you in return for your not getting vexed with me for blotting your copy-book. So now you have the cause of my willingness."

"So much for our rules!" exclaimed Giles, triumphantly. "They work to a charm."

"What rules?" inquired Lucy.

"We must tell Lucy all about it," said Giles.

They did tell her all about it; and the result was, that she agreed to join them in trying the new rules.

COALS OF FIRE.

PART I.

cous´in	**chuck´led**	**mo´tion-less**
el´e-gant-ly	**glo´ri-ous**	**hur´ry-ing**
rigged	**scam´per-ing**	**un-fas´tened**
launched	**un-ea´sy**	**doubt´ful-ly**

JOE BENTON lived in the country. Not far from his father's house was a large pond. His cousin Herbert had given him a beautiful boat, elegantly rigged with mast and sails, all ready to be launched. The boat was snugly stowed away in a little cave near the pond. At three o'clock on a Saturday afternoon the boys were to meet and launch the boat. On the morning of that day Joe rose bright and early. It was a lovely morning. Joe was in fine spirits. He chuckled with delight when he thought of the afternoon. "Glorious!" said he to himself, as he finished dressing. "Now, I have just time to run down to the pond before breakfast, and see that the boat is all right. Then I'll hurry home and learn my lessons for Monday, so as to be ready for the afternoon."

Away he went scampering towards the cave where the boat had been left ready for the launch. As he drew near he saw signs of mischief, and felt uneasy. The big stone before the cave had been rolled away. The moment he looked within he burst into a loud cry. There was the beautiful boat, which his cousin had given him, with its mast broken, its sails all torn to pieces, and a large hole bored in the bottom!

Joe stood for a moment motionless with grief and surprise; then with his face all red with anger he exclaimed, "I know who did it! It was Fritz Brown; but I'll pay him for *this* caper—see if I don't!" Then he pushed back the boat into the cave, and, hurrying along the road a little way, he fastened a string across the footpath, a few inches from the ground, and carefully hid himself among the bushes.

Presently a step was heard, and Joe eagerly peeped out. He expected to see Fritz coming along; but instead of Fritz it was his cousin Herbert. He was the last person Joe cared to meet just then, so he unfastened the string and lay quiet, hoping that he would not observe him. But Herbert's quick eye soon caught sight of him, and Joe had to tell him all that had happened; and he wound up by saying, "But never mind; I mean to make him smart for it!"

"Well, what do you mean to do, Joe?" asked Herbert.

"Why, you see, Fritz carries a basket of eggs to market every morning, and I mean to trip him over this string, and smash them all!"

Joe knew that this was not a right feeling, and expected to get a sharp lecture from his cousin. But, to his surprise, he only said, in a quiet way, "*Well, I think* Fritz does deserve some punishment: but the string is an old trick; I can tell you something better than that."

"What?" cried Joe, eagerly.

"How would you like to put a few coals of fire on his head?"

"What! *burn* him?" asked Joe, doubtfully. His cousin nodded his head, and gave a queer smile. Joe clapped his hands. "Bravo!" said he, "that's just the thing, Cousin Herbert. You see, his hair is so thick he would not get burned much before he had time to shake them off; but I would just like to see him jump once. Now tell me how to do it—quick!"

"'If thine enemy hunger, feed him; if he thirst, give him drink: for in so doing, thou shalt heap coals of fire on his head. Be not overcome of evil, but overcome evil with good.' There," said Herbert, "that is God's way of doing it; and I think that is the best kind of punishment that Fritz could have."

You should have seen how long Joe's face grew while Herbert was speaking. "Now I do say, Cousin Herbert," added Joe, "that is a real take in. Why, it is no punishment at all."

"Try it once," said Herbert. "Treat Fritz kindly, and I am certain that he will feel so ashamed and unhappy, that kicking or beating him would be like fun in comparison."

Joe was not really a bad boy, but he was now in a very ill temper; and he said sullenly, "But you have told me a story, Cousin Herbert. You said this kind of coals would *burn*, and they don't burn at all."

"You are mistaken about that," said Herbert. "I have known such coals burn up malice, envy, ill-feeling, and a great deal of rubbish, and then leave some cold hearts feeling as warm and pleasant as possible."

Joe drew a long sigh. "Well, tell me a good coal to put on Fritz's head, and I'll see about it."

"You know," said Herbert, "that Fritz is very poor, and can seldom buy himself a book, although he is very fond of reading; but *you* have quite a library. Now suppose—but no, I won't suppose anything about it. Just think over the matter, and find your own coal. But be sure to kindle it with love, for no other fire burns like that." Then Herbert sprang over the fence and went whistling away.

COALS OF FIRE.

PART II.

car′ry-ing	day′light	ap-point′ed
un-com′fort-a-ble	af′ter-noon	twin′kle
some′times	ap′pe-tite	bus′iness

Before Joe had time to collect his thoughts, he saw Fritz coming down the road, carrying a basket of eggs in one hand and a pail of milk in the other. For a moment the thought crossed Joe's mind, "What a *grand* smash it would have been, if Fritz *had* fallen over the string!" But he drove it away in an instant, and was glad enough that the string was in his pocket. Fritz started and looked very uncomfortable when he first caught sight of Joe; but the good fellow began at once with, "Fritz, have you much time to read now?"

"Sometimes," said Fritz, "when I have driven the cows home and done all my work, I have a little daylight left; but the trouble is, I have read every book I can get hold of."

"How would you like to read my new book of travels?"

Fritz's eyes fairly danced. "Oh! may I, may I? I would be *so* careful of it."

"Yes," answered Joe; "and perhaps I have some others you would like to read. And Fritz," he added, a little slyly, "I would ask you to come and help to sail my new boat this afternoon; but some one has gone and broken the mast, and torn the sails, and made a great hole in the bottom. Who *do* you suppose did it?"

Fritz's head dropped on his breast; but after a moment he looked up with great effort, and said—

"Oh, Joe, *I* did it; but I cannot tell you how sorry I am. You did not know I was so mean when you promised me the book, did you?"

"Well, I rather thought you did it," said Joe slowly.

"And yet you never—" Fritz could not get any

further. He felt as if he would choke; his face was as red as a coal. He could stand it no longer, so off he walked without saying a word.

"That coal *does* burn," said Joe to himself. "I know Fritz would rather I had smashed every egg in his basket than that I had offered to lend him that book." Joe took two or three leaps along the road, and went home with a light heart and a grand appetite for breakfast.

When the boys met at the appointed hour, they found Fritz there before them, eagerly trying to repair the injuries; and as soon as he saw Joe he hurried to present him with a beautiful flag, which he had bought for the boat with a part of his egg money! The boat was repaired and launched, and made a grand trip; and everything turned out as Cousin Herbert had said, for Joe's heart was so warm and full of kind thoughts, that he never had been happier in his life. And Joe found out afterwards that the more he used of this curious kind of coal, the larger supply he had on hand—kind thoughts, kind words, and kind actions.

"I declare, Cousin Herbert," said he, with a queer twinkle in his eye, "I think *I shall have to set up a coal-yard!*"

I should be glad to have all of you, my young friends, engage in this branch of the coal business. If every family were careful to keep a supply of Joe Benton's coals on hand, and make a good use of them, how happy they would be!

L. P.

COTTON.

dis-cov´er-y	pin´a-fores	sweet´meat
Man´ches-ter	del´i-cate-ly	stream´ing
fi´bre	gos´sa-mer	pro-pelled´
He-rod´o-tus	thun´der-ing	treas´ured
Christ´ian	ma-chines´	sup-ply´ing
cra´dled	weav´ing	man´kind

[*Dick and Nelly sitting reading. Enter Lubin and Matty.*]

Lubin. Dick, Dick, we have made such a discovery! We have found a tree that bears—lambs' tails!

Dick [*looking up in surprise*]. That bears what?

Matty. Not really *lambs' tails*, of course, but something very like them, a little longer than my hand, covered with wool so white and soft! I am sure that it must be cotton. The ground was all white with the down!

Dick. Ah! I know what tree you mean; it grows at the end of the field. I have been told that it is the black poplar. That is not a cotton tree, though it produces a kind of cotton. The fibre of this is too short and weak to make it of use for weaving.

Nelly. Where does the real cotton plant grow?

Dick. It was first known as a native of India. The writer Herodotus, who lived more than four hundred years before the Christian era, tells of the Indians possessing "a kind of plant which, instead of fruit, produces wool of a finer and better quality than that of sheep." Calico was named from *Calicut* in India. An immense quantity of cotton is also grown in both North and South America, as well as in other parts of the globe. Like the sugar cane, it requires a great deal of heat.

Matty. Is cotton the flower of the plant?

Dick. No; it is the bed of soft white down in which the dark seeds are cradled. The cotton flower has five bright yellow petals, with a dark red spot upon each. It grows upon a plant which is usually about two feet high. After the flower has dropped off, its seed vessel swells larger and larger, till when about the size of a filbert it bursts open, and the delicate cotton appears ready for the negroes to pick.

Matty. A field of ripe cotton must look as if it were covered with snow.

Dick. All cotton is not so beautifully white. You remember our old pinafores of nankeen?

Matty. They were a kind of dull yellowish buff. I always wondered why they were dyed of that colour instead of pink or light blue.

Dick. They had never been dyed at all. They were made of a peculiar cotton that grows in China, and were called *nankeen* from the city of Nankin.

Nelly. Is not muslin made from cotton?

Dick. Yes; some in India has been woven so delicately fine that it is said that a whole breadth of it could be drawn through a lady's ring!

Matty. Oh, how I should like to have a dress made of that! It must be almost like the gossamer web that glitters with dew on the field on a morning in autumn!

Dick. There is little chance of your ever wearing or seeing such a dress. The poor Hindoos, who patiently wove with the hand that delicate muslin web, have been thrown out of employ by our big machines, that do more in a day than the humble weaver then could have done in years! I wish, Matty, that you could visit Manchester as I have done, and hear the thumping and thundering of those huge machines, like iron giants at work! *In half an hour* one of them can spin a cotton thread that would reach *all the way from Manchester to India!* And as for the weaving—

Matty. Oh, I should like to know, if all the cotton brought over in one year were woven into cloth, how large a space it would cover.

Dick. If all the cotton imported into our islands in the year 1860 were woven into common print, and spread out at once over the land, it would cover *half of Yorkshire!* and if woven into the thinnest kind of cloth, it would cover *the whole of Yorkshire*, the largest county in England, containing a *city, sixty market towns*, and more than a *million of people!*

[*All the children held up their hands in surprise.*]

Dick. I'll make you open your eyes a little wider yet! Suppose that, instead of covering up Yorkshire till it look as white as a wedding-cake, we take the common print-cloth, a yard wide, and begin rolling it like a band round the globe—

Matty. I am accustomed by this time to your *going great lengths*, Master Dick; I should not wonder if you told us that it would reach right round the world, so that, wherever sailors crossed the line, they should find it made of white cotton! [*All the children laugh.*]

Dick. You think that you have gone pretty far, Matty; but you have not gone half far enough for the truth! The cloth woven from the cotton imported in 1860 would stretch *two hundred times round the big round* globe;—your cotton *line* would be *two hundred* yards wide!

Matty. Well, if ever I heard such a thing in my life!

Nelly. To think of all that cotton coming from the pods of a plant!

Lubin. What endless bales must have come pouring in at our ports in that year 1860!

Dick. Enough, if placed in a row, to extend to a distance of three thousand three hundred and seventeen miles—or nearly as far as from Liverpool to New York!

Matty. Well, I am half inclined to envy the people of America and India, they are so rich in good things. Their clothing grows on their bushes—

Lubin. And if they want a sweetmeat, why they have but to break off a bit of a cane as they walk, and they find it streaming with juice like honey.

Dick. And yet I am not sure that I would exchange our hard dry crop for their sweet one, or our black crop for their white one.

Matty. Our black crop—what can you mean? I never saw a black crop on the ground in my life.

Dick. No; my black crop is deep under ground.

Matty. Surely you must mean *coal!*

Nelly. And the hard dry crop must be—*iron.*

Dick. You have quickly guessed my riddle.

Lubin [*laughing*]. But as we cannot *wear* coal, nor *eat* iron, I think that the cotton and sugar are better.

Dick. Stop a moment, my friend. How are the rich cargoes from foreign lands brought in abundance to us? Are not the engines of steamers of *iron;* and are they not fed with *coal?* How is the soft down of the cotton plant changed, as if by magic, into calico, muslin, lace and net, and so made fit to be used as clothing? Mighty engines, formed of iron, and propelled by steam, do the wondrous work, giving employment and food at the same time to hundreds of thousands of people. We receive produce in a raw state, we work it, and then send it over the world, chiefly by means of the iron and coal which are treasured up in our mines.

Nelly. And, oh, how often have I heard my mother say how good God is, thus to divide his gifts amongst various nations; how he teaches us by this that we are intended to love and to serve one another! While we exchange goods for our profit, each land supplying the need of others, we should learn that no nation is made to stand alone, but that each and all may bring something by which to increase the general welfare of mankind.

A. L. O. E.

POETICAL PIECES.

THE PARROT.

A PARROT from the Spanish Main,
  Full young and early caged, came o'er
With bright wings to the bleak domain
          Of Mulla's shore.

To spicy groves where he had won
  His plumage of resplendent hue,
His native fruits, and skies, and sun,
          He bade adieu.

For these he changed the smoke of turf,
  A heathery land and misty sky,
And turned on rocks and raging surf
          His golden eye.

But petted in our climate cold,
  He lived and chattered many a day;
Until, with age, from green and gold
          His wings grew gray.

At last, when blind, and seeming dumb,
  He scolded, laughed, and spoke no more,
A Spanish stranger chanced to come
          To Mulla's shore.

He hailed the bird in Spanish speech;
  The bird in Spanish speech replied,
Flapped round the cage with joyous screech,
          Dropt down, and died.

CAMPBELL.

POOR DOG TRAY.

ON the green banks of Shannon when Sheelah was nigh,
No blithe Irish lad was so happy as I;
No harp like my own could so cheerily play;
And wherever I went was my poor dog Tray.

When at last I was forced from my Sheelah to part,
She said, (while the sorrow was big at her heart,)
Oh! remember your Sheelah when far far away;
And be kind, my dear Pat, to our poor dog Tray.

Poor dog! he was faithful and kind, to be sure;
And he constantly loved me, although I was poor;
When the sour-looking folk sent me heartless away,
I had always a friend in my poor dog Tray.

When the road was so dark, and the night was so cold,
And Pat and his dog were grown weary and old,
How snugly we slept in my old coat of gray,
And he licked me for kindness—my old dog Tray.

Though my wallet was scant I remembered his case,
Nor refused my last crust to his pitiful face;
But he died at my feet on a cold winter day,
And I played a sad lament for my poor dog Tray.

Where now shall I go, poor, forsaken, and blind?
Can I find one to guide me, so faithful and kind?
To my sweet native village, so far far away,
I can never more return with my poor dog Tray.

CAMPBELL.

THE DOG AND THE WATER LILY.

It was the time when Ouse displayed
His lilies newly blown:
Their beauties I intent surveyed,
And one I wished my own.
With cane extended far I sought
To steer it close to land;
But still the prize, though nearly caught,
Escaped my eager hand.

Beau marked my unsuccessful pains
With fixed, considerate face,
And, puzzling, set his puppy brains
To comprehend the case.
But with a cherup clear and strong
Dispersing all his dream,
I thence withdrew, and followed long
The windings of the stream.

My ramble ended, I returned;
Beau, trotting far before,
The floating wreath again discerned,
And plunging left the shore.
I saw him with that lily cropped
Impatient swim to meet
My quick approach, and soon he dropped
The treasure at my feet!

Charmed with the sight, "The world," I cried,
"Shall hear of this thy deed:
My dog shall mortify the pride
Of man's superior breed!
But chief myself I will enjoin,
Awake at duty's call,
To show a love as prompt as thine
To Him who gives me all."

Cowper.

AFTER BLENHEIM.

It was a summer evening,
Old Kaspar's work was done,
And he before his cottage door
Was sitting in the sun,
And by him sported on the green
His little grandchild Wilhelmine.

She saw her brother Peterkin
Roll something large and round,
Which he beside the rivulet
In playing there had found:
He came to ask what he had found,
That was so large and smooth and round.

Old Kaspar took it from the boy,
Who stood expectant by;
And then the old man shook his head,
And with a natural sigh—
"'Tis some poor fellow's skull," said he,
"Who fell in the great victory.

"I find them in the garden,
For there's many here about;
And often when I go to plough
The plough-share turns them out:
For many a thousand men," said he,
"Were slain in that great victory."—

"Now tell us what 'twas all about,"
Young Peterkin he cries;
And little Wilhelmine looks up
With wonder-waiting eyes:
"Now tell us all about the war,
And what they fought each other for."—

"It was the English," Kaspar cried,
"Who put the French to rout;

But what they fought each other for,
I could not well make out:
But everybody said," quoth he,
"That 'twas a famous victory.

"My father lived at Blenheim then,
Yon little stream hard by;
They burnt his dwelling to the ground,
And he was forced to fly:
So with his wife and child he fled,
Nor had he where to rest his head.

"With fire and sword the country round
Was wasted far and wide,
And many a childing mother then
And new-born baby died:
But things like that, you know, must be
At every famous victory.

"They say it was a shocking sight
After the field was won;
For many thousand bodies here
Lay rotting in the sun:
But things like that, you know, must be
After a famous victory.

"Great praise the Duke of Marlbro' won,
And our good Prince Eugene."—
"Why, 'twas a very wicked thing!"
Said little Wilhelmine.—
"Nay, nay, my little girl," quoth he,
"It was a famous victory.

"And everybody praised the Duke
Who this great fight did win."—
"But what good came of it at last?"
Quoth little Peterkin.—
"Why that I cannot tell," said he,
"But 'twas a famous victory."

SOUTHEY.

BISHOP HATTO.

The summer and autumn had been so wet,
That in winter the corn was growing yet :
'Twas a piteous sight to see all around
The grain lie rotting on the ground.

Every day the starving poor
Crowded around Bishop Hatto's door,
For he had a plentiful last year's store ;
And all the neighbourhood could tell
His granaries were furnished well.

At last Bishop Hatto appointed a day
To quiet the poor without delay :
He bade them to his great barn repair,
And they should have food for the winter there.

Rejoiced such tidings good to hear,
The poor folk flocked from far and near ;
The great barn was full as it could hold
Of women and children, and young and old.

Then when he saw it could hold no more,
Bishop Hatto he made fast the door ;
And while for mercy on Christ they call,
He set fire to the barn and burnt them all.

"I' faith, 'tis an excellent bonfire !" quoth he,
"And the country is greatly obliged to me,
For ridding it, in these times forlorn,
Of rats, that only consume the corn."

So then to his palace returnéd he,
And he sat down to supper merrily,
And he slept that night like an innocent man ;
But Bishop Hatto never slept again.

In the morning as he entered the hall,
Where his picture hung against the wall,
A sweat like death all over him came,
For the rats had eaten it out of the frame.

As he looked there came a man from the farm—
He had a countenance white with alarm:
"My lord, I opened your granaries this morn,
And the rats had eaten all your corn."

Another came running presently,
And he was pale as pale could be:
"Fly! my Lord Bishop, fly!" quoth he;
"Ten thousand rats are coming this way—
The Lord forgive you for yesterday!"

"I'll go to my tower on the Rhine," replied he;
"'Tis the safest place in Germany;
The walls are high, and the shores are steep,
And the stream is strong, and the water deep."

Bishop Hatto fearfully hastened away,
And he crossed the Rhine without delay,
And reached his tower, and barred with care
All the windows, doors, and loopholes there.

He laid him down, and closed his eyes,
But soon a scream made him arise:
He started and saw two eyes of flame
On his pillow from whence the screaming came.

He listened and looked—it was only the cat;
But the Bishop he grew more fearful for that;
For she sat screaming, mad with fear,
At the army of rats that was drawing near.

For they have swam over the river so deep,
And they have climbed the shores so steep,

And up the tower their way is bent,
To do the work for which they were sent.

They are not to be told by the dozen or score—
By thousands they come, and by myriads and more;
Such numbers had never been heard of before,
Such a judgment had never been witnessed of yore.

Down on his knees the Bishop fell,
And faster and faster his beads did he tell,
As louder and louder, drawing near,
The gnawing of their teeth he could hear.

And in at the windows, and in at the door,
And through the walls helter-skelter they pour,
And down from the ceiling, and up through the floor,
From the right and the left, from behind and before,
From within and without, from above and below;
And all at once to the Bishop they go.

They have whetted their teeth against the stones,
And now they pick the Bishop's bones:
They gnawed the flesh from every limb,
For they were sent to do judgment on him.

SOUTHEY.

CPSIA information can be obtained
at www.ICGtesting.com
Printed in the USA
LVHW100516130422
716029LV00002B/136

9 783752 594614